John Milne

Daddy's Girl

NO EXIT PRESS

This edition published in 1999 by No Exit Press
18 Coleswood Road, Harpenden, Herts, AL5 1EQ

www.noexit.co.uk

A CIP catalogue record for this book is available from the British Library.

ISBN 1-874061-90-4   Daddy's Girl

2 4 6 8 10 9 7 5 3 1

Printed by Caledonian International Book Manafacturing Ltd, Glasgow

To Carlo and Tyga and their family

Part One
Defoe is Dead

Chapter One

It's a hot summer's day in July and I'm on a Parisian street, heading for my hotel. The street is wide and full of noise and traffic. Cars passing throw dirt and dust and fumes into my nostrils and I don't want to be there. A young man selling newspapers in a café stares at me and I pause for a second, almost sure I know him. Then I walk on, sure I don't. He stares after me. I have a spare shirt and underclothes in a little grip in my right hand. In my left I hold a walking-stick. The handles of both make my palms sweat. My shirt is stuck to my back and my jacket feels as if it's dripping. I don't want to be there. I'm in Paris for the second time in a week and I'm thinking, why me? why do I have to come? The answer is easy . . . I need the money. I'm looking for a girl and someone's paying and I need the money.

I walked past a fish restaurant. It was closed for the afternoon but made the street stink, open or closed. There was an old-fashioned French police van there, full of young fellows with their hats cocked on to the backs of their heads and smoking French cigarettes. Puff puff, they'd get the sack in London. Past the fish restaurant deep shadow fell across the road, and I turned into a narrow street. The pavement was squishy underfoot from rubbish, restaurant debris. Grey bins and black plastic bags were at the kerbside, waiting for the binmen. *Service des ordures* is one of my few French phrases and I have no idea why I know it or where I know it from.

Outside my hotel was a load of stuff waiting for the *service des ordures*, too. I pushed through the double glass doors. In the foyer an air-conditioner made a racket but no cold air. There was a black man behind the desk and his eyes widened when he saw me.

'I booked,' I said. 'From London for the one night. I rang.'

He stared at me but didn't speak. He was small and very black, an African, no doubt. I pointed at his guest book.

'You'll find me in there. Jenner is the name. It's only two nights since I was last here.' No response. I waited for a while. 'Small world, eh? with me coming back. That Paris, it certainly gets a hold on people. I could hardly stand to stay away, y'know?'

The eyes stayed wide and still there was no reply. I turned. Opposite the desk was a little sitting-room. The door to the sitting-room was open and I was surprised to see a woman sitting there. Her hair was cut short and spiky, dyed black, and she wore too much make-up. She wore a bright yellow silk blouse and a matching skirt of some other material, and she smiled when she saw me and stood to greet me. She took half a pace forward. We were about ten feet apart, but in different rooms. I smiled too. Then someone grabbed my arms and a firm hand snatched the walking-stick from my grasp. The young woman watched from the room opposite, sinking back into her seat and staring but saying nothing. The black man stood behind his desk, rubbing his knuckles nervously. The men by my side were uniformed policemen. One picked my bag from the floor in front of the desk, then they turned me towards the street again; talking quietly, guiding me. Two more policemen were standing in the hotel doorway and all five of us marched down the road to their old-fashioned blue van. No one was smoking in the van now; no one was sitting with his cap on the back of his head. The two by my side put me in the back of the van and when the doors were closed another policeman searched me. I could feel him tense when he came to the harness for the false part of my leg, as if I was one of those flashy American detectives with a gun or a knife strapped to his calf. Well, I don't have a gun or knife strapped to *any* part of me.

'What's this for?' I asked quietly, but I only did it once and I didn't hold out much hope of a reply. The contents of my pockets went, with my weekend grip, into a huge black plastic bag already marked 'Jenner'. Someone wanted to see me. If they'd spoken English – which I doubted they did – the uniformed policemen would have confined themselves to

4

comments of the 'You'll soon find out' variety. I felt okay anyway. I hadn't done anything illegal and France is in the EEC. Why worry? What's there to be scared of? I kept telling myself I hadn't done anything illegal. Then the van pulled off and I was sitting jammed between two blue-uniformed men in the back of a French hurry-up wagon. Perhaps I should have struggled at the hotel. Perhaps I should have shouted and ranted until an English speaker turned up. Perhaps I should never travel abroad again, especially to France. I closed my eyes and tried to relax. What's to be scared of? Quite a lot, actually. There always is.

*

There are lots of different types of policemen in France, and during that evening I think I must have met most of them. It did my topographical knowledge of Paris some good and my nerves some harm. Eventually I was led by two uniformed coppers from a holding cell in what appeared to be half a town hall, half a police station (which was where my vanful of heroes had taken dangerous old me) to the street again.

'This way,' said one in English. He was a ginger-haired, mouse-faced man and I was very relieved to hear the sound of my own language at last.

'You speak English?' I asked.

'*Non*. This way, this way. You come this way.'

'Why? What am I supposed to have done?'

'You come this way.'

I went, not least because I was handcuffed to his colleague.

*

'This way' was the prefecture of police, on the quai des Orfèvres. Between the palace of justice and the prefecture (two equally imposing and dreary buildings on an island in the centre of Paris) is a road connected to a bridge at each end. I sat in a late-model black Citroën saloon in this road for half an hour or so. The ginger-haired, mouse-faced policeman was in the driving seat and his companion sat in the rear with me. Handcuffs, again. There was no radio to listen to and the policemen didn't speak to each other, let alone me. The street was broad and – at this time in the evening – quiet. I could hear the traffic sometimes, horns or roaring engines from either side of the river, and I could hear the regular clip-clip-clip of his boots as a guard with a machine-gun strolled by us on the pavement.

A man came and sat in the front passenger seat. The driver tipped his cap.

'*Chef.*' And started the car.

The man in the passenger seat was dark and slim. He was aged around forty and he wore a lightweight grey suit and a thin, tightly knotted black tie. He turned and looked at me. He was handsome, in a way, with dark, receding hair, intelligent brown eyes and that permanent half-pursed look to his lips which Frenchmen often have.

'You are Mr Jenner, James Jenner?' he asked.

'Yes.'

'Do you have papers?' He leaned over the seat-back, holding out his hand. We were cruising now through the twilight streets of Paris, heading west. We were on the southern or 'left' bank of the river and there were great buildings, government buildings to our left and a wall to our right. Couples strolled on the pavement by the wall, lovers, I suppose, and tourists. Honeymooners and second honeymooners . . . isn't that what Paris is supposed to be for?

'These guys have them. They took them away in the police station.'

The detective nodded and turned his back to me. 'Do you know where we're going?'

It didn't deserve an answer and I didn't give one.

'I am Letellier. Inspector Letellier. And you and I, Mr James Jenner, have some business together.' He said this with his back turned still, speaking to the windscreen. We were passing bridges all the time and there were no walking couples here. The bouncing soft yellow headlamps of the cars around us shone into the Citroën. Letellier opened his side window. 'It's too hot, Jenner. Too hot. Don't you think?' He translated the sentence for the driver without waiting for me to reply. The driver nodded and wiped his brow to prove it.

We stopped outside another official building, this time near the Eiffel Tower's complex of parks and wide streets. A short fat man wearing – even on this hot evening – a loose gaberdine-type mac jammed himself into the car beside me. No one spoke more than a couple of muttered words. We drove on.

6

This time we crossed the river. After a few more minutes we stopped outside a gateway in a wall. The street, compared with central Paris, was almost suburban; full of leafy gardens and substantial houses behind tall walls and railings. One toot on the Citroën's horn and the gate opened, then I was led by the policeman named Letellier and the short fat fellow into a low building full of the familiar neon light and squeaky linoleum. A sign on the wall urged caution with *la rage*. Quite right too. Also there was a smell, a hospital smell. The place didn't feel like a hospital, though.

'In here,' said Letellier.

'What's this?' As if I needed to ask. A morgue. Row on row of filing cabinet drawers, big ones, against a wall. The air was chilly and there were clean white mica-topped tables in the middle of the room with lamps and hanging microphones over them and clean mica gutters for blood to flush into. There was plenty of light.

The fat detective had my walking-stick, my black plastic bag marked 'Jenner' and another black plastic bag in his hand. He handed me my stick.

Letellier pulled a drawer open.

'Know him?'

He drew back a white, semi-opaque nylon cover, revealing a young man. The young man had unruly, black curly hair and his face was unshaven. His dark eyes stared straight ahead, unseeing. His skin was ghastly white, except his left temple, which was crushed. His left eye stared out of a bloody compounded mess.

'I don't know him.'

'We think you know him,' said the fat detective.

'Not me.'

'We think you might have murdered him.' His face was nearly as ghastly as the corpse's, and only slightly better shaven. The detective was balding, and he scratched his head through the thin brown hair and said, 'We have good evidence, anyway.'

'I don't know him.'

The fat detective flapped his gaberdine mac, as if to let some of the mortuary's cool air circulate around his body. Then he dipped into an inner pocket and produced a small clear plastic bag with a piece of card in it. He held the bag out between finger and thumb so that I should see the card.

7

'This is one piece of evidence, anyway. We have others. Okay?'

It was my card, with the name of the hotel written on the back in my own hand.

'*Met* him. I've *met* him. But I've never actually spoken to him. I certainly don't know him, and as for the card . . . well, I give lots of them out.'

The fat detective pointed into the drawer.

'You gave this one to him three days ago. People saw you, anyway. You hired a car. The car was seen outside his house. Then he was found dead.'

'It's a long story.'

'You had better tell us your story. Sit.' He pointed to a hard, wooden-seated chair, the type you only find in government-run places, England or France.

'Tell us.'

The short detective patted me on the shoulder as I sat, then laughed heartily. Letellier smiled.

'What's the joke?'

'No joke. Tell us.'

'I have nothing to hide.'

'So, Mr English Investigator, begin your story.'

I began to speak.

Chapter Two

Paris is not, of course, my natural habitat. London is. I live in north-east London in a flat in Stoke Newington. If you hang out of my kitchen window you can get a 'glimpse' of Clissold Park. If you look below – still hanging out of the kitchen window – you can see where buses and milk carts and people pass. Not too many taxis, since the denizens of my quarter are none too well off and don't have much call for taxi rides. That's the kind of place I live in.

If you look below my kitchen window about two in the afternoon you will see a strange sight. This is the guided tour of Stoke Newington, begun, I presume, by some well-meaning person in the leisure services department of the borough council. On summer afternoons a trail of wide-eyed foreigners – usually Americans – follows an attractive young woman guide along Stoke Newington Church Street. She points out the fine council meeting house on one side of the street, she points out some other stuff (I know not what, I haven't taken the tour) on my side of the street, and then she stops outside my flat and they all rest on the little wall by the car-park and the local muggers eye them up while she says, 'And this is where Daniel Defoe lived during his time at Newington Green Academy.'

But where does she mean? Not my block of flats, Defoe Mansions, which were built in the thirties and look it. Not nearby Defoe Road, which was built a long time after his death. There's little in Stoke Newington that isn't either Victorian or later, and if Defoe inhabited any of the houses you can see from the street below my window he must've lived a very long time. About two hundred years should do it.

The young lady from the borough council solemnly indicates the car park to my block of flats and says 'Daniel Defoe lived here' and no one thinks to contradict her. The visiting foreigners all nod solemnly and etch the patch of tarmac where Defoe lived in the 1670s in their memories. Then, two years later when their grandsons come home from school in Lancing or La Jolla or Laredo all full of Robinson Crusoe the grandparent can say, 'Oh, *Defoe*. Yeah, Defoe. I was outside his house on my trip to Europe.'

'Really, Grandad? Outside his house?'

'Sure was.'

But he wasn't. He was outside mine. And when the guide lady finished feeding him false information he went in search of a taxi he couldn't find and he didn't take his hand off his wallet till he got back to the comfort and safety of the Penta or the Hilton where they know how to make a Martini and there's a rank of cabs right outside the front door. He doesn't tell his grandson that and I don't blame him. It would spoil the story.

The guide lady started her trips in March, which was a little ambitious, really, and she wore a heavy blue coat and was accompanied by other Defoe-seekers in heavy coats. By April she was in a snappy blue proofed-cotton topcoat and she wore something resembling a British Airways stewardess's uniform under it, right down to the little red neckerchief. Maybe she worked for an airline and Defoe-seeking was a side-line. Maybe she just invented the Defoe story to make the tour more interesting. One thing is certain about the guide lady... she never comes without an umbrella. Winter, spring, summer; in Defoe country the rain keeps coming. The better advised of her clients carry umbrellas, too. I can look down from my kitchen window at the scabby tarmac-ed car-park, at the little red-brick wall, and the middle-aged heads and raised umbrellas. I watch the rain fall on them all and know; Defoe never lived *here*.

Chapter Three

When the English summer comes the rain still falls – but it's warmer. Lucky us. I sat in my old Rover car opposite a second-hand car lot in the Romford Road. The warm rain fell steadily on my Rover and my breath fogged up the windscreen. I couldn't use the fan to clear it, either, because my car takes so long to start that the battery's permanently run down. I wiped the screen with the back of my hand and watched a young man on the car lot. He was standing under an umbrella with a middle-aged woman and I had no doubt at all he was telling her that *this* grey Ford Escort of approximately one year's vintage was better than *any other* grey Ford Escort of one year's vintage and that she would be a whole lot better off buying from him than any other used-car man because he had his company's long-standing reputation for honesty to keep up. The young man and the middle-aged woman climbed into the Ford Escort. The next time I looked up the windscreen had misted over again and they were gone. I wound down my side window and leaned my temple against the cool, chamfered edge of the glass. *Gilligan, Gilligan, Gilligan* screamed brightly painted red and white signs above the car lot. Since 1947 Now Three Generations. Our Word is Our Guarantee. Check Gilligan's Price First. Best Trade-Ins In Town. Any Inspection Welcome.

Buses passed, sloshing rainwater under their tyres. The Ford Escort came back and parked in front of the car lot, this time with the middle-aged woman driving. The young man took her into the car dealer's office, then came out immediately, alone, and crossed towards me. He was in his mid-twenties, slightly

11

built, and he was wearing a smart, sharply cut blue suit. He held a pale-grey rainproofed-cotton trenchcoat over his head and shoulders. He didn't look the sort of man who would like getting his blond hair wet.

'Jenner?' He stood next to my open window.

'That's me. You must be Mr Gilligan.'

But he was already walking round the back of the car. I let him in. Gilligan threw his coat back off his shoulders as if it was a mantle, then shivered.

'Got them?' I asked.

He pulled a waxed-paper package from his side pocket and threw it on to the dashboard.

'Is that the lot?'

He nodded. 'You talked about a fee.'

I stowed the package under my seat.

'You don't need a fee, Mr Gilligan. I'm sure you were pleased to help.'

Gilligan's sharp grey eyes focused on mine for a moment. 'We had a deal,' he said.

'I just told you money was a possibility. That's all. We didn't have a deal.'

Gilligan thought about this for a long time, then he said, 'I've kept two. Just in case you welched on me.'

I patted his arm. He flinched.

'You're no blackmailer, son. You're honest. I asked you for them and you've given them to me.'

'I've kept two. How was I to know I could trust you?'

'Your face is too honest for a car dealer ... anyone tell you that?' I leaned across him and pushed the door lever.

'I need the money, Jenner. I'm not the car dealer. I'm the office boy. It's my father's business. And I'm serious. I have kept two letters in a safe place and I want money for them. Tell him I'm desperate.'

'I'll tell him. I'll tell him not to pay, too. Is that your father?'

A small dark-haired man stood in the doorway of Gilligan's office and stared across the road at us.

'Tell him I want money.'

'It's not a question of money. Perhaps you should ask your father.'

Gilligan got out of the car and stood in the rain. He didn't seem to care whether he was wet now. His young face twisted in

12

anger. He leaned back through the open door and said, 'He's a bastard and you are too.'

I looked at the dark-haired man in the doorway.

'Which he?'

But Gilligan had gone.

My car didn't take more than half a dozen goes to start. I should have got him some money, young Terence Gilligan, and then he could have done me a deal on a used Ford Escort. Best Trade-Ins In Town. Check Gilligan's Price First. Knackered Old Rovers Taken In Exchange.

*

In Stratford I parked on a double yellow line and rang my client.

'Mr Tiler? George Tiler?'

'Yes.'

'Jimmy Jenner here. I've got your stuff.'

'Any problems?'

'No.'

'All there?'

'I don't know. You'll have to say. I'll bring them round tonight and you can see for yourself.'

'I'm having some people round tonight.' He was silent, then, 'Yes, why not? You come too. Come over to my flat at nine.'

'Well, if you've got people there I don't know how we can discuss this business.'

'What's there to discuss? I'll know if it's all there or not. See you tonight.'

And he hung up. Back at my car a traffic warden was writing a ticket.

'I've got a "Disabled" sticker,' I said.

'I can't see it.'

She was a profoundly plain young woman with mousy hair in a pony tail and dull brown eyes. I could see I wasn't going to like her. Her mouth set and she kept writing.

'It fell down. Look, it's on the floor.'

'It should be firmly affixed to the screen. That's the regulation.'

Scribble, scribble, scribble.

'But now you've seen it,' I said.

'I'm already writing your ticket. You'll have to take it and write in to explain.'

'Write in' was a magic phrase and simply saying it seemed to give the mousy meter lady some pleasure.

'I'm *disabled*.'

She looked sternly at me. 'You don't look so disabled that you can't write a letter. Perhaps you're not entitled to that sticker.' She ripped the perforated ticket from her pad. I ignored it and pulled my trouser-leg up. From the knee down the right leg is not the original Jenner.

'That's very impressive,' said the lady traffic warden. But she still gave me the ticket.

'I was a police hero. That was me. I've got commendations and I've lost my leg.'

'Buses have to get through here. You're lucky it wasn't towed away... and then where would you be?'

'Stratford?'

Chapter Four

George Tiler's 'people round' ran to about five hundred, with catering to suit, and I really wouldn't have been surprised to find the Rolling Stones or somebody doing the floorshow. He even had large men in monkey suits at the door with a guest-list. George was *rich* and his friends reckoned themselves *chic* and they were damn-well making sure everyone knew it.

George (I mean, that's the second thing he says to everybody, 'Call me George', whether you're working for him or not) owns a flat which is a whole floor of a converted wharf building down in Ratcliff. When I arrived the ape on the door had my name and told me to 'Come right in' . . . as opposed to 'Piss right off', I presume.

'Fix yourself a drink,' said the ape, waving across the mob. I did. I went to a bar about the same size as you'd find in a pub and helped myself to a very large glass of whisky. The party was a party party, not a talking one, and the room was hot and sweaty with heavy beating black American music glued to the walls and sticky-looking white people glued to each other; girls' hair plastered to their heads, boys' shirts stuck to their backs.

'James.'

George Tiler appeared at my side as if he'd come out of the floor on a lift. He was wearing a pale-grey Nehru suit and looking pleased with himself.

'Hello, George.'

'James, I want you to meet Tony and Louise Frames-Pargeter.'

He stepped aside as a magician might to reveal a florid-faced man in a pin-stripe accompanied by a woman who was too fat and wore pearls to match. The smallest pearl was a marble and the biggest a gob-stopper. The man had white hair and the woman would've too, if she hadn't been dyeing it honey-brown.

'Hi. Er, George, can we talk? I have...'

But George tugged my sleeve.

'Tony's a political agent.' He turned and beamed at Tony. 'And James is a private eye.'

'*How* interesting. I've never met one before.' Tony and Louise spoke at once and then giggled. 'Really,' Louise said, trying to sound earnest.

'Really. What does a political agent do, take ten per cent off the top?'

And they laughed in unison; a worthy, hollow-sounding laugh. This 'pleased to meet you' double-act was well rehearsed.

'Do you mind if I circulate, folks? It *is* my party,' said George, and promptly did it. Tony and Louise Frames-Pargeter stayed for a few more polite seconds, as a political agent should, and then pulled the same stunt. They never looked more foreign than a couple of Martians, say, or the boy and girl from Atlantis complete with pet codfish. I couldn't imagine why George had asked them to his party. Since he didn't take his letters or talk to me I don't know why he asked me either. I patted the letters in my pocket and downed the Scotch. I was wondering whether to have another and go or plain go when a woman turned from a group of trendies haw-hawing next to me and said, 'Are you one of George's friends?'

Which could have meant 'Are you another shirt-lifter?' or 'What's a scruff like you doing here?' By the time I cleared my throat she said, 'Well, who cares anyway? What's your name?'

'Jimmy.'

She smiled and held out her hand.

'I'm Leila Lucas. I'm in publishing and we're doing a book of George's . . . George Tiler, it's his party.'

'I know. What's the book about?'

'Inner-city blight . . . he's an architect, you know.'

'Of course.'

Tony and Louise were doing something resembling Chubby Checker's twist in the middle of a throbbing mob of young people.

'Do you dance?'

'No. What did you say your name was? Serena?'

16

She shook her head. 'Leila.'

Well, they all work in one of the media businesses and they're all called Cassandra, Alexandra, Selina, Serena and Leila. Perm any two from five. This particular Leila was five-ten or so with black, bob-cut hair. She was good-looking in a way that used to be called vivacious and she could claim to do anything she wanted for a living, it was okay with me. Saying you're a private detective sounds imaginative, too. I told her that later. I'd teased her a lot in between.

'How do I know this one is true?'

'Scout's honour.'

'That's no use. You lie.'

'White lie.'

'So how do you know George? I don't think he normally mixes with private detectives.'

'Who does? Not me,' I said. 'I'm the only one I know.'

'Really?'

'Really. Let's have another drink.'

'Really . . . a private detective. You're my first.' She rubbed her chin thoughtfully. 'I might have some work for you.'

'Not for me you don't.'

'I'm sure.'

'Blow in my ear first.'

She said, 'Give me your card.'

'This place is boring, Leila. Blow in my ear and we'll dump your friends and go off and have supper together somewhere. Somewhere quiet.'

'It's not boring now. Give me your card.'

I gave her my card. She blew in my right ear there and then, which is about as prompt a payment as you'll ever get.

Chapter Five

Nobody becomes a private detective so he can earn peanuts and act as an unqualified pseudo-bailiff for anyone with fifty quid in his pocket . . . nobody except a dimbo, that is. When dimbo-Jenner became an investigator he expected to do more than look for run-away husbands, more than squeeze penny-ante insurance claims. He didn't expect to start at the top, but he expected to go up-market pretty soon. Seven years into my career, here is Jenner's recipe for going up-market and mixing with a better class of person: (1) go home drunk at night; (2) wake up late; (3) answer telephone; (4) voice says 'Jenner, we need you.'

On a day like that I should be backing ponies or dealing in stocks and shares . . . 'Sell yen and buy dollars, Jenner in London is selling yen and buying dollars.' Only my day like that was a Sunday.

A late May dawn Sunday. At least it's dawn if you're hungover and your eyes are slits and the fellow in the next block whose flat backs on to yours chooses this Sunday, just this Sunday, to put in his new German kitchen. The Tannhäuser Küchen . . . all you supply is the drill, the screwdriver and a quiet Sunday morning. Brr, wake up, Jenner. Brr.

I stumbled out of bed and put the coffee machine on, then sat naked at the kitchen table reading the colour supplement to my newspaper. I'm never going to afford a new BMW, I know, but I read those ads and weigh one car against the other as if it's an issue I have to resolve before lunch. Sod it, I'll hire a chauffeur and let him choose, leaving me to concentrate on the city pages.

18

The phone rang and the coffee machine finished together.

'Jenner,' I said, tantalised.

A nasal, upper-class English voice came flooding out of the earpiece.

'Slow down, miss. Slow down and start again.'

'My name,' she said, as if she was speaking to a moron, 'is Caroline Chumley-Smaithe . . . got it?'

'Ten four.'

'I'm Leila's immediate superior.'

'Leila?'

This held her up for only a second.

'I think you've met,' said Caroline Chumley-Smaithe. 'She told me you worked for George.'

'Not me, lady. I work for myself.'

'*Had done* work for George. I wanted to know how much you'd charge to look after something of a star of ours for a few days.'

'What time is it?'

'Time? Ah . . . eleven. Just coming up to.'

I could smell that coffee. A tall gorgeous blonde held open the door of a Japanese sports car while a line of type said it had special brakes. The man next door started up his drill again.

'Let me phone you, miss . . . what is it again?'

'Chumley-Smaithe.'

'Let me phone you back.'

*

When I rang back I'd had a chance to remember not only where I got the hangover but who I got it with.

'Depends. What "star" and what does "look after" mean?' I said.

'Can't you just give me your rates?' said Caroline Cholmondley-Smythe (which – I discovered later – is how you spell Chumley-Smaithe).

'I charge a hundred pounds per day plus expenses payable in full on completion or whenever the bill reaches five hundred pounds. Whichever's the sooner. But I still have to know exactly what you want and I still have to decide whether I want to do it or not.'

There was a silence, then Caroline Cholmondley-Smythe said, 'We're doing a book by Charles Wallace. He's an actor.'

19

'Never heard of him.'

'That's hardly the point, Mr Jenner. He's an English actor who's lived in America for absolutely years and has written a novel which absolutely exposes Hollywood.'

'He's a *film* star?'

'TV. I'm sure you'll recognise him. We'd need someone to look after him, get him around town, all that,' Caroline said through her upper-class twang. When 'town' hit her tongue it became 'tie-yn'. Her Jenner was 'Jannah'. 'You'd be in charge of organising transport and fending orf unwanted reporters. Just for this week. We'd pay three hundred pounds.'

'Five plus expenses.'

'From today until next Thursday.'

'Done.'

Which was my mistake. I should have gone and looked him over first. I should have insisted on that at least. My trouble is, I hear an accent like Caroline Cholmondley-Smythe's and I immediately think they speak the truth, the whole and nothing but the. Well, Caroline didn't. She never mentioned, for example, that I'd spend the entire week pulling the fat oaf out of drunken fights, nor arguing him out of his tenth whisky for lunch, nor listening to his mind-numbing anecdotes hour after hour. She never mentioned either that I'd have a ringside seat at one of the world's best displays of hypocrisy, with Charles Wallace fawning over every Grub Streeter who came his way and then giving out what arseholes they were as soon as they'd left. No, Caroline spoke with forked-tongue, and instead of sitting there with my mouth open thinking what a lucky fellow I was and wasn't it nice I was beginning to catch a better class of trade, I should have been considering the fact that nobody pays five hundred quid for nothing and nobody calls in a rubbish collector unless they have rubbish to collect. What kind of man needs someone to organise his taxi rides and drive him round London? A numbskull or a drunk, that's who. Either way, he was going to be at least five hundred quid's worth of trouble to me.

An hour after Caroline Cholmondley-Smythe rang I was on my way to Heathrow to meet a Pan Am flight. I stopped at Charing Cross and posted George his love letters, plus my bill plus a note explaining that Terence Gilligan claimed he was short of money and wanted to know if George could help him out to the tune of a grand or so. Apart from writing 'This is what happens if you continually write letters like that to your men friends, George' I don't know how I could have made it any clearer. Not everyone would let himself be bullied the way I'd bullied Terence, and if George wanted to stay gay, publicity-shy *and* an avid letter-writer he would have to come to terms with the fact that one day someone was going to take him to the cleaners. It's a conclusion he would have to reach for himself, though.

Chapter Six

The following Thursday night I was sitting in the bar of the St John Hotel, Piccadilly, and I was looking forward to my cheque. Every evening that week I'd looked forward to my cheque. I could have earned that money easier coal-mining.

'They all stink,' Charlie Wallace said. 'What do they know about people like me? They're all time-servers, waiting for their pensions. Slinging expense-account gin down their throats all day. Everything's at someone else's expense.'

Charlie lit a cigarette, fumbling the packet through yellow-stained fingers. He held the first lungful down for an age, then spoke out clouds of smoke. 'They make me bloody angry.' He puffed quickly at his cigarette to demonstrate how angry he was. 'The whole bloody stinking business sticks in my throat and it stinks.'

Wallace didn't look like a TV star. He was very short and quite fat, with a round, red, dry-skin and burst-blood-vessel face. Bright white grizzle hair showed on his chin and cheeks where he'd shaved erratically. The hair on Wallace's head was very white too, and had deposited a fall-out of dandruff on the upper part of his double-breasted blue suit.

'I accept that I'm in a disreputable business and I'm a sort of disreputable fellow. Well, I accept it.' He sucked at his whisky glass and paused, inviting me to disagree with him: like a thin girl who tells you she's fat and gives you a chance to say, 'No you're not.' I didn't want to argue with Charlie Wallace, though.

'But my God there's a *grand* dishonesty about that lot and

their treatment of people like me. It's nearly as poor as . . .' He shook his head slowly. 'It's so poor I can't even think of anything it's as poor as. I'm defeated by it . . . how about that?'

It would have been something if I'd never heard the speech before. I sighed. He ignored my sigh. I stretched and yawned, saying something about the room being 'close'. Wallace kept talking. He never seemed to notice whether anyone was listening or not.

Outside the summer had started for real. Outside was a summer's evening with orange evening light and traffic and dust. I wanted to be outside. After a week, I just wanted to be where Charlie Wallace wasn't.

'How about that, they defeat me for words?' he said again. I just looked around the bar. It was modern designer-plush, kitted out with plenty of velour and the kind of waiters who would give even obsequience a bad name; men who wore clip-on bow-ties and would rush over if they even caught you glancing at them. Congenital lackeys.

'Where's my bloody girl, Jenner?'

'I don't know. They gave me to understand she was due. What does she look like?'

'*Why* don't you know?'

'Because I never met her.'

He frowned for a moment, then shook his head. 'Why don't you know where she is? And what's all this prissy "they gave me to understand"?'

I stared resolutely at the curtain and thought not just of my cheque but of cashing it. One hundred blue fivers stretching up the beige velour curtain one after the other. Wallace drank from his whisky glass again and aired his raucous Anglo-American accent.

'It stinks. Now I know why I left this country. Because it stinks. Those borgy bastards live like ticks on the backs of people like me, borrowing our dreams. Who appointed them in charge? I hate them all.'

Borgy was a new one.

'What does "borgy" mean?'

Wallace didn't seem to hear. A very young woman had come into the room. Wallace stood up yelling, 'Over here, over here.'

The very young woman smiled in return. Heads turned to follow as she walked to our table. That girl was a traffic stopper. She was a natural blonde with cool regular features and smooth skin. She looked about eighteen and when she kissed her father she winced a little and when she shook my hand she allowed her ash-grey eyes to meet mine for just a second. You wouldn't need many looks from those eyes to get you jumping through hoops or whatever else she wanted. I wondered if she knew... of course she did. From about the age of four beautiful women know what it does.

'This is my daughter Lenny. And Lenny, this is my babysitter, Mr James Jenner, late of the Metropolitan Police. He's a private detective. He's been hired to make sure I get around this city safely. Isn't that nice?'

I unlocked my jaw and said, 'Pleased to meet you.'

If she was aware of herself she didn't play on it. Wallace's daughter just sat there like any old plain Jane.

'Lenny Wallace,' her father said, 'is short for Eleanor. And "borgy" is short for bourgeois.' Then to Eleanor, 'Our friend here has a very literal turn of mind. And not much humour.'

The young woman said, 'Only my father calls me Lenny. It's a childhood name.'

'Whatever you say...'

'Hey!' Wallace called. A young Greek or Cypriot waiter rushed over as if we were drowning and he was the only swimmer in the room.

'I want another Scotch and these two miseries should have some wine before their faces get permanently fixed like that... champagne, I think. Does this dump stock champagne?'

The waiter nodded and began to speak but Wallace was too fast. 'Okay, okay, does a pig snort? Don't start recommending, just bring us one. Where's the bloody wine list?' He waved his hand before the waiter could make it back to the *maître d*'s table. 'Don't worry, don't worry. I don't want his opinion either. Just bring us the most expensive champagne you have. Only the best for Charlie Wallace and his guests. You know Jenner here, and this is my daughter, Lenny.'

The waiter smiled nervously at the unexpected introduction. Eleanor Wallace smiled nervously, too. I wanted to say 'I don't want your champagne' but I didn't. I looked at the girl, but she said nothing. She worked her knuckles on her lap, though, and she looked awfully tired suddenly for one so young.

Chapter Seven

Wallace passed out at nine-thirty. A waiter and the hall-porter carried him to the lift, all the time making out he'd only fainted. The waiters cursed and I limped, a scene we'd done every night that week except I had a beautiful young girl on my arm and she was shrinking the shoulder of my good suit with all her tears and leaning against me and quivering and saying, 'What should I do?' Since Charlie had administered the night's local anaesthetic and would now cause problems exclusively of the snoring variety, the immediate answer was 'Relax, Eleanor.' For the longer term, say tomorrow, I didn't know. Charlie was her problem and no one seemed about to employ Jenner as their live-in Filipino-boy . . . which job Jenner wouldn't have considered anyway.

'Put him to bed,' I said, 'and then go on the town for the evening. Do you know his doctor?'

She shook her head. 'I don't believe he would have one in England. I don't know about New York.'

'Get him one in London. Ask the hotel management. Ask Caroline Chumblybumbly. Get a quack to come and see him and talk to him. Don't try and do it all alone. Do you have friends in England?'

'Some. France mostly. I went to school there. I've never really lived in America with him.'

'Use them. You'd be surprised how people respond to a call for help . . . gives them the chance to act the Samaritan. Can I take it you don't have any plans to go back to America with him?'

'You can.'

'Well there you go. He's only here for another week at the most. Just see him for a couple of hours a day. Go off and do things on your own.'

'Here,' she said. We were at Charlie's room. The door was open and the waiters were muttering inside. 'Mine's opposite.' She was holding my hand and smiling a little now. 'Should I go out straight away or wait a while?'

'I don't know. Your father, your life. You decide. I think he'll be okay.'

'Would you leave?'

'Yes.'

She nodded slowly. 'Okay. I don't have anything specific to do.'

I hesitated. I'd done what I was hired to do. I'd got Charlie to his appointments on time all week. I'd delivered him to his daughter in the St John Hotel, Piccadilly, alive and well (relatively) just as Caroline Cholmondley-Smythe had required. We had come to no arrangement for late-night working, overtime or pastoral services to troubled girls.

'You'll find something,' I said.

I should've walked out right then, but instead I gave Eleanor my card and said, 'Give me a ring tomorrow night and let me know how things are. He's not going to be any problem now, at least.'

Then I was out of the St John Hotel as fast as any man with just the one leg could and I was flagging down taxis and whooping along the street like a kid at the end of term. I had nothing other than sympathy to offer Eleanor, really. Her father was her problem. If Eleanor needed a break from that fellow *she* would have to make it.

The best thing she could have done would have been to get right on the street beside me and start flagging her own taxis. She should never even *look* leave alone *go* back. You can't tell a young person that. They have to work it out for themselves or it's no use at all. I strolled along Piccadilly and only felt the tiniest bit guilty. I had a date for a late supper in Gerrard Street with the lovely Leila, and the prospect soon put Charlie Wallace and his daughter out of my mind.

Chapter Eight

The next day I slept in. At ten Leila called her office and told them she was working at home for the morning. She didn't specify the home. I lay with the sheet over my face protecting my delicate complexion from the morning sunlight and feeling happy. It was a good day. I had a girl by my side. I had a cheque for five-seven-two smackeroos (includes expenses) winging its way to me by the Royal Mail. There was a bit of rare English summer weather to greet Jenner whenever he wanted it and most, *most* important of all, there was no prospect whatsoever of my having to look at Charlie Wallace's ugly mug or listen to his big mouth all day. Bliss. At ten-oh-five the doorbell rang.

'Jenner.'

'It's okay, call me Jimmy.'

'Oh . . . Jimmy. Can I talk to you?'

I was standing in carpet slippers, pyjama trousers and an ancient brown itchy-wool dressing gown. Eleanor Wallace was on my doorstep wearing a white cotton designer suit and looking about to cry again. She looked very vulnerable. I yelled, 'Well, you'd better come in, Eleanor,' so loudly I'm surprised she did it, but Leila took the hint and stayed in the bedroom while Eleanor sat on my beaten-up sofa and told me all about it. There wasn't a long and complicated story. Eleanor was just at the stage in life where your parents seem to be selfish ratbags and the future – at least on the emotional front – looks at its bleakest. Everyone gets it to an extent, but in Eleanor's case it was the A1 guaranteeable truth that at least one parent wasn't interested in

27

the world outside himself. The mother had had it away on her toes some years ago and – according to Eleanor – was last heard of breeding sheep in Argentina.

I made tea. Eleanor told me all about how she'd been schooled in France, how she only knew her father from school holidays and even then each time she saw him it would be with a different woman, possibly living in a different home and always with a bottle of Scotch open. The women seemed to last only slightly longer than the bottles of Scotch. Charlie sounded a real beaut of a parent. Dr Spock eat your heart out.

'What do you want from me?'

She crossed her legs and pouted. There were damp tracks of tears on her face. 'I suppose I should simply *be* with him . . . but I just don't want to. It doesn't have to be my responsibility, does it?'

'Drink some tea.'

'Well, last night had me thinking. You know?'

'No. What?'

'That I should leave.'

'I know you were thinking about that . . . but you'd only just arrived. Maybe he'll get better.' Even as the words came out of my mouth I was thinking, 'No he won't, what a stupid suggestion.'

'You think I should just stick it out for a few days?'

'Uh . . . I didn't say that.'

'You think I shouldn't?'

'I can't tell you. You have to say.'

There went those tears again. I said nothing more for a while, then she said angrily, 'It's ridiculous. A grown-up man shouldn't need it.' And she snuggled up next to me and said through sobs, 'What should I do?'

'Leave,' I said straight away.

'You think so? Just leave?'

'That's right. Isn't it what you wanted to hear?'

She nodded.

'Where'll you go?'

'I can stay with a friend in France for a few days, then I'll go on . . . I don't really know where. I've got a flat but I don't want to go home.'

We sat in silence for a while, then she said, 'But what about Charlie? He has nearly another week before he goes back to New York.'

28

'The rest of his life starts here. He can't always have been like he is now.'

Eleanor stood and rummaged through her handbag.

'Look, I've brought this.' She held out a bundle of cash; all twenties it looked like. 'I wondered if I could convince you to take over.'

I shook my head.

'It's five hundred. Isn't that enough for a retainer?'

'Where'd you get the cash?'

'I've got cash, don't worry. Is it enough?'

'It's not a question of enough. You can't spend your life hiring private detectives to accompany your father everywhere in case he gets so sozzled he dies. Sounds tough but that's what it is. You want me to look after him for the next couple of days so that if he falls under a train you don't have to spend the rest of your life feeling guilty. Eh?'

She didn't answer.

I picked the bundle of money from her hand and waved it at her.

'I'll do it. I'll take your money and I'll do my best to look after him. But grown-up life starts here, Eleanor, so let's just be clear about what you're buying. You're using me to buy off your conscience. Lots of people use men like me in that way . . . but they have to be clear that *that's* what they're doing. Look, five hundred quid . . . I cost a hundred a day plus expenses. You can get someone cheaper if you want, you know?'

She nodded but said nothing.

'I'll take it out of this and send you the rest. How about an address?'

'I'll give you one.' She stood close to me. She held her face up to me and it looked for all the world as if she was waiting for me to kiss her. I gave Jenner a mental black mark for even considering such cradle-snatching and said, 'I'll deal with him. Where is he now?'

'Sleeping. He doesn't have any appointments until lunchtime, then he's going book-signing in Hatchard's.' Another sob, but less enthusiasm than before.

'Just go. Live your life . . . that's what you want to hear, eh? Do what you want. Pay cash and do what you want. There's a pad over there. Write down this friend's address in France and then you'd better go. I'll have to get dressed if I'm going to Hatchard's.'

29

'Thanks.' She kissed me very lightly on the cheek. 'Thanks a lot, Jimmy Jenner.'

*

'That little minx,' said Leila, 'simply wanted to get her own way. She was using you.'

'Of course.'

'She's so selfish towards him. She didn't want to do anything for him to start with and now she's wriggled out of the little bit she agreed to do. Her selfishness is why you were asked to do this job in the first place.'

'That's right. Your boss employed me solely to help out Eleanor Wallace. She's a big-hearted woman.'

'Don't be sarcastic. Couldn't you tell she was using you? Girls like her do.'

'Of course she's using me. I told her so.'

'Don't be smug. That doesn't stop it being a fact. She just wants to get off and bang some spotty teenage boyfriend. She was using you to get away from Charlie.'

'Wouldn't you?'

'Oh, Jenner . . . that's rich!' She grabbed the lapel of my dressing gown. 'Are you accusing me of something?'

Leila and her boss both knew they'd use me to save themselves spending too much time with old best-seller-big-mouth-take-the-lid-off-Hollywood-Charlie. They wanted the money his horrible book would make but they didn't want Charlie, and though they'd paid me it wasn't the straightest deal a man was ever given.

'I'm accusing you of nothing. But I just told the girl I would help her and I've taken her money on the bargain. I'd better get to work.'

'No you're not, Jenner. Not yet. You have a bargain you struck with me, too. I cancelled a morning's work for you.'

She let go of the lapel and held out her hand. I took it.

'It won't take long to get there by cab,' she said.

'I'll be late. I'll feel guilty.'

'It's guilt that makes it best of all. Guilt's the seasoning.'

'Philosophy too. I didn't count on philosophy.'

'Well, there you are.'

And she was right. There I was.

A real detective, the professional of my teenage dreams,

would have had a tough moral code to which he could adhere under all circumstances. Like the Scotland Yard detectives in Edgar Lustgarten movies who won't accept a drink because they're 'working'. Or like E. Zimbalist Jnr.; a character with a set jaw, a sense of justice and a really thick sidekick. It's not easy to have tough moral codes, though, and even harder to keep to them. We'd all save ourselves a lot of grief if we had a rule book for all circumstances and needed only to refer to it to figure things out. I would have done, that day. But it was a warm May day. The world was full of light and the sap was rising for the summer. Leila was wearing one of my old shirts and not a lot else. If she was willing to put off whatever the hell she did for an hour I should be willing to put off pounding the streets of London. The work could wait. Charlie could wait . . . even Charlie could get from one end of Piccadilly to the other in safety, surely. Then I'd find him in Hatchard's and drag him off for a late lunch. The worst that could happen would be if Charlie found Hatchard's fiction department's emergency gin bottle and ended up autographing copies of *Jane's Fighting Ships* and making a load of leery remarks through boozy breath at the sales girls. The absolute *worst*.

I should get one of those strict rule books and stick to it, that's what I should do.

Chapter Nine

Not only could Charlie not get from the St John Hotel to
Hatchard's – a distance of less than five hundred yards – in
safety, he couldn't get out of the hotel's revolving door without
breaking his spectacles. He had to have a porter fix them with
Sellotape and it's surprising how rare rolls of adhesive tape are
in Piccadilly hotels. By the time they'd sent out for some and
fixed the spectacles Charlie was late for Hatchard's. Charlie
went out and hopped on the platform of a number twenty-two
bus that was cruising slowly towards Piccadilly Circus. When
Charlie tried to part company with the bus by the same
unconventional method he fell and broke his right leg. I know,
because Caroline Cholmondley-Smythe told me through a
hysterical voice she'd nearly got under control. 'And I can't find
the daughter who's supposed to be looking after him, Jenner.
She's just vanished. I can't find my bloody assistant, either. I
wonder, could you, just for today...'

'He's here for three more days,' I said.

'I'll find the daughter by tonight. I'll have Leila come and let
you know what's happening this afternoon. If I ever find her.
You'll be in the hotel?'

'Presuming they'll let him out of hospital, yes. I guess so.'

'Oh they'll let him out, Jenner. They'll let him out.' And then
she muttered, 'As if I didn't have anything else to do.'

'His book must be worth an awful lot to your company,
Caroline.'

Suddenly, savagely, she said, 'It's rubbish. It stinks and I
bloody-well hate it.' And slammed the phone down. I guessed
that meant 'yes'.

'If I were you,' I said to the figure slumped over my kitchen table, 'I'd go down to the London Library and look like you'd been there all morning. Then I'd casually call your boss and hold the phone about a foot from your ear and say, "How's things?" Okay?'

The answer, which was a long time coming, was 'Ugh'. I was limping downstairs when she yelled, 'What happened?'

'Top secret. Better that you know nothing. Just phone your boss. You know nothing and you haven't seen me nor Eleanor Wallace today. Slam the door hard when you leave, eh?'

In the street some socially deprived teenagers were eyeing my old Rover. They're easy to pinch, the locks are no good. I didn't shoo the boys away and they didn't even bother to look ashamed, they just strolled off and gave me sullen looks while they did it. The street was hot but my car was an oven. The heat hit me as a wave when I opened the driver's door. I opened all the windows to let it cool, then sat behind the steering-wheel with my eyes closed. I was thinking that I get involved too easily and I was trying to compose myself for the day. Sweat ran down my brow, dripped off the end of my nose. I could feel it on my collar, too. My lips tasted salty. When I drove off the teenagers were back in their own car, a Mark II Ford Cortina with a mauve fur interior and a power bulge riveted on to the bonnet. None of them was a day over fifteen and they stared right back at me and their stares were a challenge that I didn't take up.

*

The hospital kept Charlie Wallace for three days with his leg in the air and they gave him tea and water to drink. Nothing else, no matter how hard he screamed. They tut-tutted at his body the way a mechanic would if you ever let one get his nose under the bonnet of your car. Charlie needed his crankshaft reground and a new set of rings. He needed gaskets all over the place and he was smoking and using a lot of oil. 'Well, not round here he's not,' said the bone-doctor – or something like it – and they fed him tea, water, soup and that was *it*.

'One dry bread roll a day and a lot of lip about "How did you ever let yourself get into this condition?"' said Charlie when I went to see him. His foot was raised, there wasn't a cigarette in the building and he'd been reduced to reading back copies of *Reader's Digest*.

'Did you know, Jenner, that the Canadian moose...'

'No and I don't want to. I'm taking you to Heathrow in the morning so you can go and get your body purged by some other tyrant in New York.'

'Thanks.'

'It's okay.'

Charlie's hospital room was just off the Euston Road; private, expensive, triple-glazed and utterly without character. I pushed the blind slats apart so I could see my car in the street. Even the orange 'disabled' sticker doesn't save you from clamping round there.

'What time?'

'Eight-thirty. I'm accompanying you in the ambulance.'

He grunted and tossed his head on the pillow. 'Just to be sure I'm gone?'

'Something like that.'

Charlie's nurse came in to plump his pillows. She was small, neat, Chinese-looking and very attractive. When she left I said, 'That's what you get on the BUPA, eh? Pretty nurses.'

'I don't have BUPA. I'm paying.' He was silent for a moment, then said, 'Who's paying you?'

'Who do you think?'

Charlie rubbed his face and laughed. 'As long as I'm not.'

'Just have your bag packed in the morning, sweetheart.'

'I think it's my daughter. So she doesn't have to look after me and so she doesn't have to suffer the guilt of knowing no one is.'

'Wrong. It's Caroline.'

'Why should she? I've done what I came here for. Why should she care what happens next?'

'Okay, I admit. It was the favourite auntie who always took you out to tea when you were a schoolboy, away from the freezing dormitory and the advances of your housemaster. It was me, because I care for you so much and couldn't stand the thought of you being in pain and forgotten with only a pretty Chinese nurse to while away the hours with. And your auntie and me, we split the cost with this Canadian moose you've been reading so much about in the papers.'

He turned his face into his pillow as much as the suspended leg would allow and spoke obscenities. I clicked the door softly closed behind me.

*

34

Two days after Charlie had taken off from Heathrow – and ceased to be any responsibility of mine – a tall skinny example of the genus 'upper-class twit' came round to Defoe Mansions and said, 'If you don't stop seeing her I'll break your legs.'

'I don't know who you mean,' I said – truthfully.

'My name's Tommy Lucas and I'm here to tell you that if you touch my wife again I'll break your legs. Just leave her alone.'

He was all blazing blue eyes and sharp-looking bones and he didn't laugh one bit when I said, 'Leg. You mean leg in the singular. If I keep seeing her you'll break my *leg*. The lower part of this one has taken an early bath in the great football match of life owing to its having been blown off by protesting Arabs. Bad luck on me, eh? Tommy?'

Which seemed to faze him, since bashing up blokes with just the one leg is way outside the rules his lot go by. He contented himself with a lot of violent finger-wagging and some *just-you-make-sures*. He didn't need to worry, anyway. I called at her Chelsea flat a few days later and discovered Leila had acquired a bricklayer from Muswell Hill with tattoos and big muscles for the tattoos to go on, with a hairy chest and a broad enough cockney accent to satisfy *all* her friends. He never spoke much, but then I don't suppose that was the point.

'Leila, you're a real brick,' I said and waved goodbye. The bricklayer flexed a few tattoos and growled. Tommy Lucas wasn't going to break any of *his* legs, either.

'I'm not coming back,' I called from the safety of the street below her window. 'You'll all just have to manage without me. I'm going back down-market. I'm going back to the insurance claims and disappeared husbands. They need me.'

Which, like much in life, was nearly true.

Chapter Ten

Early July and I'm in the posh flat of George Tiler, architect,
letter-writer, patron of one-legged detectives. He'd had me
recover not one but *two* lots of letters he'd written temporary
pals, and the second lot dated back to 1967. I took this bundle to
George's flat, sat on his big plump sofa, looked into his big
plump face and said, 'George, why?'

'Why?'

'Why am I chasing your old letters? It's crazy. More to the
point – why write them?'

George buried his head in a newspaper. Suddenly the centre
pages of the *Telegraph* had become very important.

'You don't like people having them and it's costing you the
earth to have me get them back.'

No answer, then George slapped the paper down on the sofa,
beside himself.

'Look at this. It's obscene. Three murders on one page. That's
really disgusting, don't you think?' He pointed to a page he
hadn't even been reading. There was a report on a railway
guard who'd been stabbed by a drunk, a child who'd been
throttled by its own father, and an Italian politician who'd been
shot dead. Since the politician wasn't English and wasn't on an
English street we were treated to a picture of the corpse, face
down at some foreign kerbside. He looked for all the world as if
he'd lost a contact lens.

'*That's* a scandal, James. That people should feel able to do
these things to each other. *That's* a scandal. It happens around
us every day. It's happening now!' His voice was outraged. I
didn't doubt he was honestly outraged.

'Last Sunday. Before then, even. Not now.' I pointed at the paper's date. 'Give me a reason for the letters, George.'

He stood and walked to the end of his massive living-room. George swung open one of his panoramic windows and leaned out.

'Don't lose your hat, mate,' I called. 'I'm not going after it.'

George clutched at his hat. I'd called just as he was about to go out for the evening, so fat George was dressed in a very large leather version of a bus-driver's outfit, complete with a bent-up and silver-studded leather busman's cap which he was now holding firmly to his head. George waved his free hand at the city and the river below him. 'What's it all for, Jimmy? Why do people bother?'

I stood by his side and looked over the council estates of Deptford and Rotherhithe. Awash with orange light, they seemed so calm and quiet.

'I don't have a clue, cocker.'

He turned and smiled. 'Style . . . it's all for style. All the rotten concrete estates, all the places like this,' and he slapped his hand on the huge and ancient wooden beam that was his panoramic window's sill, 'are designed for a purpose. And part of that purpose is a sense of style. It might seem incidental, just part of the surface look, Jimmy. But it's not. It really matters. And that's how things were with me. It used to be my style to be completely over the top, the letters as well as all sorts of other passionate declarations. It's what the whole business is about. It's my personal style.'

'Is?'

'*Was.* Now I'm a reformed character.' He laughed at the idea.

'Why the sudden rush to have all the letters back then? Why are they a threat? Are you considering marriage?'

He laughed again.

I said, 'I'm right. Why does your past have to be such a secret? Is it the daughter of a duke?'

'No duke's daughters, I promise.' George squeezed up his face like a man who'd just eaten a lemon. 'I can't bear people having that stuff unless they're in love with me too.'

'That's not enough, George. You managed to bear it for twenty years. Why become sensitive all of a sudden?'

'Oh, that lot's housekeeping. It was Gilligan who got me so upset about it all. He wanted money from me.'

'Bull, George. He wanted money *after* we offered it to him. I

37

mean it's all bloody mad anyway... you're paying me small
fortunes to go dashing all over the country looking for twenty-
five-year-old blond factory workers called Bill who happen to
have declarations of eternal love in their hip pocket signed
"George Tiler". I have been given bizarre jobs before but this
takes the biscuit. Tell me why I'm doing it.'

'Are you saying you won't help any more?'

'I'm saying *be honest* with me. This has gone on for long
enough.'

'Are you frightened of me, Jimmy?'

'Oh cut it out. I'm frightened of *them*. There are a lot of
twenty-five-year-olds in this country called Bill and it's no
picnic sorting out which ones are of your persuasion. I'd like to
know the truth about why I'm doing it.'

'It is the fear then. You don't want to do it in case someone
gets upset and beats you up.'

'*Of course* I don't want to get beaten up! Do I look barmy?'

'That's the seasoning, Jimmy. The thing that makes it really
exciting.'

'I should cocoa it's exciting, George.'

'For me, not you. A few guilty secrets... where would life be
without it?'

'Safe. Life would be safe and quiet. I can hardly wait until it
is.'

He crossed to a roll-top desk and ran up the shutter.

'I've got to go out. I'll pay you now.'

He wrote me a cheque, then put some cash in an envelope.
'I'd also like you to deliver this to Terence Gilligan. It's just to
help him.'

'Don't be daft.'

'Please, Jimmy.'

'Send him a postal order. Come on, I'll give you a lift.'

It took me an age to walk down the great stone steps in
George's wharf building. Neon lights lit us greenly, green men
running pursued by green flames pointed to emergency exits. I
thought of Leila and her 'seasoning'.

'Have you seen Leila Lucas?'

'Of course. She's got herself an Italian count.'

'She's a contessa?'

'No one's that dumb, Jimmy. She's the count's live-in lover.
Concubine. He's old so I don't suppose there's much
concubinage involved.'

38

'Why did she do that?'

He rubbed his fingers together. 'I'm guessing, but I don't suppose her job pays more than pocket money. Have you met her husband?'

'Of course.'

'He threatened suicide when he found out. He stalks her.'

'Someone ought to.'

We'd reached the street. Upstairs was prime real estate, downstairs prime mugging-country. Dickens-land...whenever I go to Wapping or Ratcliff I keep expecting the Artful Dodger to come round the corner singing a selection from Lionel Bart.

'Over there.' I pointed at my old Rover automatic.

'I met a friend of Leila's who said we should all look you up. Eleanor Wallace.'

'Oh yes.'

'Her father's the actor...'

'I know.'

'I've got a copy of her father's book upstairs if you want to read it.'

'Yeah. Some time. Why don't you all come round and have a party, you should have done that.'

'Stalked by Tommy.'

We'd reached Tower Hill. Evening gloom had come and streetlamps were flickering into life. Cars revved at the traffic lights, waiting for a racing start. A City of London bobby walked along Tower Hill, overlooking the moat, making sure no one stole the railings or took the Queen's name in vain.

'Where are you going, George? Up west? Over the bridge?'

'Charing Cross. Straight along the Embankment will do fine.'

Charing Cross indeed. Where else? When we got to Villiers Street it was full of down-and-outs swaggering along the line like generals, sorting out who should have the prime spots for the night's kip under the arch. The whole place stank of grease and piss and unwashed sewers. The night was throbbingly hot. Murders and fights happened on nights such as this. I told George to empty his pockets.

'Why? I never bring more than a few pounds. No credit cards. Nothing. I've been mugged once. That was enough.'

'Empty the pockets, George. Put it all up on the dash.'

George was true to his word. A notebook, four fifty-pound notes and two twenties (which George thinks is not much money). Some loose change, a comb. And two biros. I nabbed the biros.

'This is what I was after.'

'Huh?'

'The biros, sport. I'm putting myself out of work.'

In the hands of a man like George the pen is a dangerous weapon. He laughed and slapped the newspaper I'd left on my dash. 'You want them for your crossword.'

'It's not for my crossword. I hate crosswords. Go on.'

George shoved his junk back into the pockets of his leather busman's outfit and stepped out of the car. As he started up the street he called, 'I only write them in the cold light of day.'

'I'll be round at noon, George, check your outgoing letters. I'll save you a fortune.'

I opened the newspaper. It's true, I do hate crosswords. I can't do them. To do crosswords you need a lot of information in your head. Types of apples, the names of Scottish lochs, the names of famous cricketers and all the bones in the human body. You need to know the county towns of England and the names of the states in the USA. You need to know the names of Napoleon's marshals, all twenty-six of them. I hate crosswords because I'm no good at all that stuff. Ney, St-Cyr, Soult and that's my lot. Murat, that's four. Was Junot ever one? I don't know and I'm never going to look it up, either. A pre-World War I state now part of Yugoslavia? Reuben's assistant? A good-looking outlaw? Anatomy and football combine in a Scott?

Hopeless. I threw the pens out of the window, into the gutter. Within seconds one of the down-and-outs had them in his hand and was stuffing them into a huge plastic shopping bag containing God-knows-what. Now containing God-knows-what and two biros. I flipped through the pages of the newspaper. A couple of days is a long time in newspapers. The railway guard had been shunted off somewhere, the child throttled by its father was buried and the father charged. Even the big cheese Italian politician only rated an inside page paragraph on how he'd been holding the party together and all that caper. How we miss them when they're gone, those politicians. 'Mr Di Nemico was shot just twenty-four hours before he was due to meet M. Mitterand, the French President. Red Brigade Terrorists called a radio station in Milan claiming responsibility. In London, the Labour Party Leader said...'

40

something exceeded in its inanity only by the statement of another politician.

What was the name of Napoleon's secretary? Wasn't he a marshal? Was Bernadotte one? I knew them all once because our history teacher at school was mad on French history and taught us them.

I turned the car round and drove slowly back to Stoke Newington. I had George's envelope of money in my pocket for Gilligan, but I wouldn't try to deliver it until the next day. I didn't want to deliver it at all. Courting disaster, George was; just like my history teacher. One boy's father came in and yelled at him for teaching us that Waterloo was a glorious defeat to the French. 'Unpatriotic' he called it, and our history master poo-pooed him, but he didn't keep banging out the names of French marshals and French battles after that. We moved swiftly over to Chartism and you'd hardly have noticed us changing gear. Peterloo was nothing like as controversial and seemed further away.

Poniatowski. . . he was one. Poniatowski the lancer. Prince of Poland and Marshal of France.

Chapter Eleven

One of the great advantages of working at home (which I have to do now that my turnover doesn't warrant an office anymore) is that you don't have to rush out at any particular time in the morning. If you were a lazy kind of man you could be lazy. Very lazy. I'm medium lazy, which means I get up when I have to and when I don't have to I suit myself. The disadvantage which more than compensates for the freedom to indulge laziness is that your home telephone doubles up as a work one. You cannot escape your home calls at work and you cannot escape your work calls at home. An auntie will call to discuss your cousin's acne while you're waiting to close a deal; or worse, some dowager's secretary will call and ask would you find the love of the dowager's life for her, a stable boy she hasn't seen for sixty-one years and she wants to see once, just the once, before she dies. This last happened to me, it really happened, and it was ten o'clock at night and I had a visitor and we certainly weren't watching TV or anything like it. No, she was sitting on the sofa and she was nearly on fire when the phone rang. At about the tenth ring I gave up and answered.

'Jenner.'

'Oh, Mr Jenner. I expected to get an office answering machine again. I rang yesterday. Let me explain...'

And he did, whether I wanted to let him or not, and it took about fifteen minutes to get to the stable boy, by which time my visitor was well and truly doused and thinking of watching 'Mid-Week Sports Special' or whatever it is girls watch when they've gone off the entire idea.

'Can I get this right? You think that this stable boy would be seventy-six if he was still alive?'

'Minimum, Mr Jenner.'

'So what's the urgency? And why ring me so late at night?'

'My employer is a very old lady, Mr Jenner.'

'And?'

He paused, then said quietly and confidentially into the phone, 'This is a matter in which discretion is everything, Mr Jenner.'

Which must make him the zen secretary. I found the stable boy in Hounslow ... or to be more accurate I found his entry in the Register of Deaths at St Catherine's House, Kingsway, and a quick phone call to his next of kin (a sour-sounding middle-aged man in Edgware) established that his dear old dad had indeed gone to the great big stable in the sky in 1962 and was now the sole tenant of a hole in Hounslow. No, he never remembered his dad being a stable boy, he'd always been a bus driver except during the war when he'd been a tank driver. I charged the zen secretary two hundred and fifty pounds for this information which he could have acquired for himself via a bus ride and a couple of phone calls, and he seemed very pleased indeed with the deal.

'Were you discreet?'

'Excruciatingly. No one knows. She was a lot older than him, wasn't she?'

'My employer is eighty-seven.'

'Stone me! Must be all that fresh air and horses.'

'Discretion, Jenner.'

He'd misplaced my Mr, but I didn't mind. He was paying. I didn't even point out that at the time his employer fell in love with her stable boy he was sixteen and she twenty-seven. She'd been married less than a year.

Charlie Wallace was another problem caused by not having an office. If you have an office you always have the option of not being there. It's easy, even if you're there, to have some dragon on the phone fending off unwanted callers. But when your home is your office you've absolutely got to turn up at some stage, rinse out your smalls, have a sleep and a shave. Charlie rang me the day after I'd talked to George the architect. It was late in the afternoon. I was sitting at my table with George Tiler's envelope of money in front of me. I was trying to decide what to do. The best thing for George would be if I held it for a couple of days, then took it back and said, 'I can't find him.' Second best would be taking it back and saying, 'I'm sorry, George, but I can't do this for you.' Worst of all is that I should give the money to Gilligan. If Gilligan has nothing on George it would make him think George was a soft touch. It would ruin his self-respect and it would eventually lead to a great big problem for both of them. If, on the other hand, Gilligan *did* have something on George, paying him the money would make him a criminal, make him think George was a soft touch and eventually lead to a great big problem for both of them. Only lawyers would do well out of it.

The phone rang.

'Jenner.'

'Jimmy. Hello! It's me.'

'Who's "me"?'

I put the money in my 'guilt' drawer, with a load of unpaid bills to keep it feeling virtuous.

'How are you? Tell me how you're doing.'

'I'm fine. *Who* are you?'

'It's me, Charlie Wallace.'

'Hi, Charlie. What do you want?'

'I need to have a talk with you, James. Can we fix that?'

'No. I don't think so.'

'Just a talk.'

'No.'

'Well, Jimmy, it's only a few minutes and I'll pay for your time. Why don't you come over, let me give you lunch.'

'No. Is that all, Charlie?'

'It's ...' there was a long pause, 'it's very important to me that I see you. It's very important to me ...'

'Everything's very important to you, Charlie. But not me. Bye now.'

I put the phone down and turned the answering machine on. I watched the flashing lights and heard the clicks as Charlie had four more goes at impressing me with whatever was important to him, then I trooped downstairs and hailed a cab. I spent the evening getting canned in a drinking club in Frith Street, Soho, which wasn't how I'd intended passing the evening. Another disadvantage of working from home ... sometimes you've just got to get out.

*

44

I got home at two in the a.m., slightly sozzled and determined not to listen to any answering machine messages nor read any notes pushed under my door. There was a great big fellow sitting on the stairs to my flat reading a copy of the *Standard*. Train Rapes Man Held. Thatcher Says No Surrender. Plus Fashion And More. The great big fellow folded his paper and stood.

'Mr Jenner?'

'That's right.'

'Come on, then. I've got my car out there...' He began to walk past me.

'Hang on a minute.'

He was huge and ugly and unshaven, with a smashed nose carelessly stuck on his face and a slept-in look to him. He wore baggy jeans that just about held on to his hips and a floppy, thick sweater, even on this hot summer's night.

'We'd better get a move on. I've been waiting for ages.'

'What's your name?'

The great big fellow paused for a second, frowning, then said, 'My name isn't your problem, mate. It's not part of the deal.'

'Where are we going?' I measured myself up against him. He was big and ugly but he looked soft, the kind of slob they hire to keep order in dance halls. No one should be scared of him.

'Mayfair. I was told to bring you to Mayfair.'

'*Who by?*'

'I dunno. Some geezer who phoned and said he wanted you picked up. Don't *you* know who? It's common enough.'

'Not with me. Where are you from?'

He was through the communal hallway door now, holding it open for me. My brain was beginning to get itself a little straighter, too.

'*The minicab office*... where do you think I get my jobs from?' He rolled his eyes as if he'd been talking to a real fool, some dummy who doesn't understand a damn thing. That's what he thought of me. I went out to his 'minicab', a beaten-up Austin Princess, and we established over the radio that the cab had been ordered by a Mr Wallace, and the driver had been told simply to wait until Jenner came and then bring him to Wallace's house. The cost didn't matter.

'Have you got a return number on this?' I asked the cab driver, who asked his controller who asked someone else by his side. They gave me the number. I told the driver to push off and marched upstairs to have my telephone row with Charlie

Wallace. Inside my front door was a large brown envelope and it was stuffed full of money. And a note...

Jimmy... please come over and see me, any time of the day or night. I very much need to talk to you. The enclosed is a downpayment and I'll lay on transport. Charles.

I pushed the note and the bundle of his money back into Charles's brown envelope. Then I threw it across the room, walked to the sideboard and poured myself a Scotch. No ice. Who ever has ice made except regular entertainers, people's mothers and real determined drunks? I don't come into any of those categories. I put the whisky down unfinished, grabbed the brown envelope and went downstairs again. The rough-looking Austin Princess was still there and old ugly-mug, its driver, was standing under a streetlamp, smirking and smoking.

'They said to hang on. They said you'd be down again. They talked to the bloke in Mayfair on the blower.'

'You'll get mugged if you stand around like that, clever clogs. Get in the car.'

'No one will mug me, Mr Jenner. I can well look after myself.' He pulled himself up to full height inside his baggy jumper, dropped his cigarette and rubbed his nose. '*Well* look after myself,' he repeated. My reply was a little rough on the man, who was after all only providing the wheels. Why should his fantasies make me angry? They didn't, of course. Charlie Wallace made me angry. Charlie Wallace could afford to drop bundles of notes on my hall carpet, Charlie Wallace could afford to have someone like the minicab driver waiting outside my flat for a month if he felt like it. If he really wanted to be persistent I had to talk to him. Or not answer my phone or not go home for a month . . . which would effectively put me out of business anyway. It was that simple. From Charlie's point of view it's the advantage of being well off. From mine, it's just one more disadvantage of working from home.

Chapter Twelve

Charles Wallace couldn't have changed more if he'd been painted green and mounted on a marble plinth. He'd lost a couple of stone, had his hair cut neatly, was perfectly shaven and did not smell of alcohol. He did not bump into any furniture nor fall over, either. In fact the only eccentric thing Charlie did during my visit to his Mayfair service apartment happened during my first few minutes there. He pointed to the darkness beyond the window and said solemnly, 'The Queen Mother goes to church across the street. I've seen her.'

Charlie may have been right, but it's odd to think someone as grand as the Queen Mum goes to Mayfair every Sunday and rubs shoulders with the *hoi polloi*, however rich.

'I can't offer you a drink, Jimmy, I haven't got any.' Charlie eased himself into an armchair and swung one blue-suited leg over the other. 'But you can smoke if you want.'

'I don't.'

Charlie pursed his lips and nodded slowly. 'Of course. I'd forgotten.'

He was immaculate. Neat, hand-tailored double-breasted suit. Silk tie, crisp shirt collar. Charlie had sorted himself out, and the result was impressive. He looked better than *any* man ought at that time in the morning.

'Don't pull any more stunts like that taxi, Charlie. I might forget my manners.' I threw his large brown envelope into his lap. 'It's a new development in my life. People keep giving me money. Extraordinary. Yours is all there, I haven't touched it. I'm seeing you under sufferance.'

'Duress.'

'Whichever you want. I'm not volunteering. I'm here because you forced me and I'm seeing you for free, so let's get it over with. It's nearly three a.m.'

'I had to talk to you. *Had* to.'

'Talk.'

He took a deep breath and said, 'It's my daughter, Eleanor. You met her.'

'I did. I remember her. Go on.'

'She's disappeared. I don't know where she is.'

'Well, Charlie, the last time I saw her she had just that in mind...'

'Oh yes, then...' he interrupted impatiently. 'She went *then* okay. She went off with some kid.' He stood and opened his hands at his side, reminding me he was an actor. 'But this is *now*. There's no blame attached to you about that business, either.'

'You're kind... how about you?'

'Please. Just listen. I haven't seen her since we three were in that hotel. *Hadn't*, I should say. Hadn't clapped eyes on her once. Not once.'

'Charlie, I put you on a plane for New York. If she didn't go to New York also you're not going to see her, are you?'

'I was only there a week. Then I came back and got this place. Rented, you know?'

'*No?*' I'd never seen a more obvious rented place in my life. The furniture was renting furniture, only it was repro-antique renting furniture, owing to the flat being in Mayfair and probably costing as much per month as I would earn in a year. 'No shilling gas meter, though?'

He walked to the window overlooking the Queen Mum's church.

'I didn't see her even once till last week.'

Charlie was obviously wounded by the thought, as if he were some clergyman whose daughter had done a bunk with the poor box and the organist. There are no limits to the self-delusions parents have with regard to their relationships with their own children. I sighed and asked, 'What happened?'

'Why did she leave? Oh... I don't know. Some sort of teenage *Weltschmerz*, I put it down to. Isn't that normal in a girl of her age?'

'Charlie.' I stood by his side. 'Don't bring me round to your house at three in the morning just to serve bullshit. You know

48

why she was avoiding you, I know why she was avoiding you. The whole bloody world knows. You were a drunken heap who couldn't remember where he was most of the time. You are not the best example of how to be a young woman's father I have ever seen. In fact, people will probably write textbooks and case histories based on you. So don't bullshit me, because I'm tired and I want to go home . . . the question was "What happened?" and I am not bloody-well referring to things I already know. I mean "What-happened-why-am-I-here?" '

Charlie sat again. He seemed to fade into the chair. 'During the last twelve months or so, since my daughter left school, she's been bumming round Europe.'

'Why bumming? She doesn't seem short of money.'

'Hanging round with a bad crowd, slumming, spending all her money on boys and noxious substances, got it? Shall I spell it out?'

'Do.'

'She had some boyfriend in France, I knew about that. When I came to England to promote my book which takes the lid off . . .'

'Yeah. Can all that, chum. What *happened*?'

'Last week she simply turned up. I hadn't heard from her nor seen her since May, but four days ago she turned up on the doorstep and said could she stay for a few days. I was pleased, of course. I said yes.'

'How did she look?'

'Thin. Too thin. She's always been thin. She was worried, too. Worried like hell. Wouldn't open the door, jumped out of her chair every time the phone rang. Spent most of her time peering round the curtain at the street outside.'

'What's there to see in the street?'

'A confectioner's, a jeweller's . . .'

'The Queen Mum's church.'

'Right. And the pavement. That's all there is. She was looking for someone on the pavement.'

'Who? Harry Lime?'

'I don't know who. Then she left.'

'How many nights was she here?'

'Just one. She came Wednesday evening and left on Thursday mid-afternoon. I went out shopping to Fortnum's. When I came back, she'd gone. I was going to cook supper.'

I looked up at Charlie's fake chandelier. The ceiling was

stained brown from tobacco smoke, years of it. The fake chandelier hadn't been washed since Edison invented it. The room was full of fake antique furniture covered in make-believe velvet. Charlie-the-newly-reformed-drunk had offered to cook her supper here. I wouldn't have been surprised if she'd been sick on the spot.

'So she went off again?'

'Yes.'

'It's not much of a mystery, is it Charlie? She had it away from you, she came back. She didn't fancy what she saw, she had it away again. What do you want from me?'

As if I needed to ask. Miracles is what he wanted from me; find her, bring her back, make her love him like he'd been the good old dad she'd always wanted, is what Charlie wanted from me.

'She was frightened. I know it. All the time she was here she was frightened of something. Then she ran off. I think she's in trouble.'

'You fantasise she's in trouble. Then you can help her. Her only trouble seems to have been *you*.'

'You should have more respect for your clients!' he roared.

'Glad to see you're still alive, Charlie. For a minute there I thought I was talking to a cardboard cut-out of you. For your information you're not my client and your money's right there on the sofa beside you to prove it. Have you talked to the police?'

'Yes.'

'And?'

'Not the slightest interest. She's over the age of majority, doesn't even live in this country on a regular basis. They asked was I alleging she'd been kidnapped or come to any harm... of course the answer's no, I'm not alleging that. But I think she might be in some danger.'

'Fantasy again, Charlie. You'd like to think she was in some danger. It's dramatic. What you really want to do is talk to her, right?'

'Right.' He nodded slowly. 'I *do* want to talk to her. I want to know she's well. But I'm convinced she's frightened of something.'

I looked at him for a long time. He was shaky but it wasn't booze-shaky. 'Got any coffee here?'

'I'll make some.'

'A hundred a day, I charge,' I said. 'Plus expenses. Reasonable expenses. Do you have a car?'

'Downstairs in the garage.'

'Okay, Charlie. Make some coffee. That's what I want, coffee. Then tell me all there is to tell on young Eleanor. Then drive me home. Tomorrow I'll see if I can't find her and persuade her to give you a call. That's all I can promise... deal?'

'Deal. I'll give you the address of the flat she owns in Paris.'

'She's *there*?'

He shook his head. 'Hasn't been there for months. I've already had a friend check.'

That was too easy, of course. He went into the miniature kitchen and fussed around with the cupboards. I stared at the smoke-stained ceiling and tried to recall Eleanor's face precisely. It's hard, even with a woman as striking as Eleanor.

'Do you have a recent photograph?' I called.

'No,' he called back from the kitchen. Pans crashed. He came in bearing two cups of coffee. It was the worst, bitterest coffee imaginable, the kind of stuff they serve if you're ever stupid enough to ask for instant coffee in an Indian restaurant.

'Do you normally make your own?'

'I have a lady who comes in and does the meals. I only ever make tea with tea bags. Don't you like it?'

'It's fine, Charles. It's fine. I'm rather tired now, do you mind running me home? I'd take a cab but it's plain murder getting one to go further north or east than Islington.'

He laughed. 'It's vile. I think so too. Take this.' He threw the envelope back to me. 'Covers you for a week plus plenty of expenses. I know, I already asked Caroline. Just find her for me, please? Have her call me.'

'We'll see.'

*

I got Charlie's book. There was a pile a foot high by the front door and a cardboard box of back-up supplies. We limped downstairs.

'How's your leg, Charlie?'

'Could be better. I'm suing London Transport. How's yours?'

'Very funny. Where does your daughter get her money from?'

'A bank.'

'Even funnier.'

*

51

'She has a trust fund her grandfather set up for all his grandchildren. He died just after she was born and so did my marriage to his only child. Eleanor is the sole beneficiary. She has no shortage of money.'

'No chance of finding where she's drawing her cheques?'

'And doing what, staking it out for a month until she draws the next one? I hired you for your intelligence, Jenner.'

'Cheers, Charlie.'

We were swerving all over Clerkenwell by this time in Charlie's brand-new Ford Escort auto. Maybe he needed to be drunk to drive straight. Clerkenwell's not on the way from Mayfair to Stoke Newington, either, but I didn't want him paying attention to the route . . . just driving seemed to be all he could handle. If we missed north London altogether I could always take a cab instead – *if* I could find one.

'I meant we could deposit a letter with the bank.'

'Good enough.' Charlie looked at me and gave a bollard a nasty scare. White-faced passengers stared at us from within their brightly lit night bus. They probably thought we were a couple of drunks who'd stolen the Ford. 'Except I've already done that.'

'Slow down. Traffic lights, you know?'

'Good enough,' he said again.

Chapter Thirteen

I had to sit up all night. Four a.m. is too late to go to bed and I wanted to be bright and sparkly at six a.m. I amused myself by reading part of Charlie's book. Caroline Cholmondley-Smythe was right, it stank. It was in the form of a novel about six hundred pages long. Thinly disguised Hollywood persons lusted after power, money, blood and sex. Not necessarily in that order. If that's taking the lid off Hollywood they can keep it on. Also there's nothing more demoralising than reading about these thinly disguised characters without being able to rip the thin disguise off even one of them. It makes me feel so stupid. No, Charlie's book wasn't much good as books go. It was big enough to make a reasonable-sized footstool or if you had two you could balance your car on them while you changed a tyre. It sold in its hundreds of thousands, so there must be hundreds of thousands of people with more stamina than me. At least.

At six I took down my French phrase-book from my bookshelf, dialled Paris and said, '*Est-ce que vous êtes Madame Juliette Saint-Croix?*' Using up some twenty per cent of my French vocabulary. From then on it would have to be phrase-book.

'You sound as if you're English,' answered a voice which might have come from Henley-on-Thames.

'Thank you,' I said, and meant it. I closed the phrase-book. 'I'm sorry to have called so early, I just wasn't sure of catching you at home.'

'I was already up. It's seven-fifteen here, Mr...'

'Jenner.'

53

'Mr Jenner. What can I do for you?'

'I'm looking for Eleanor Wallace. Her father wants to contact her. Some weeks ago when I had to send her some money she gave me your address, so I thought you might know where she is.'

'Right city, wrong number, Mr Jenner. I'll fetch you the phone number to where she's staying.'

As simple as that. As easy as finding dead stable boys. I rang the second number and got a fellow who could (or would) only jabber in French and I couldn't thumb through the phrase-book at anything like the speed he was jabbering. I called Juliette Saint-Croix again.

'Have you been ringing the right number?'

'No doubt,' I said. We checked.

'Is it her house?'

'No. It's her friend's. Maybe his English isn't that good. I don't know him.'

'And she's definitely staying there in Paris?'

'Oh yes. I have an appointment with her tomorrow here in the city. Shall I give her a message?'

'You certainly can, Miss Saint-Croix. Tell her not to leave town without seeing me, okay?'

Chapter Fourteen

That evening found me winging my way into the Charles de Gaulle airport, a nice little place knocked up from a hundred miles of clear perspex, some underground-railway type escalators and a few dozen surly French coppers. There are no signs in English and if you ask the surly coppers they claim not to be able to speak English. Maybe they can't. I find it easy to upset French policemen and not that difficult to upset your French man-in-the-street.

I booked into an hotel my ex-wife recommended to me. It was at the far end of the rue de Rivoli (except that the far end isn't called that) and when I came out the evening was warm and sweet-smelling, with people outside cafés and leaves on the trees and plenty of bright lights shining in the street, even though it was not yet dark. I took a cab over to the left bank and strolled with the crowds up Saint-Michel; tourist crowds, mostly, but not unfriendly for all that. Lots of youngsters in sandals and jeans. Lots of sten-gun toting coppers to see us all across the road and make sure nobody mugged us.

Juliette and Eleanor's meeting was due to take place in a little bar behind the Pantheon, where there's a student quarter of sorts and little cafés offer fixed-price meals. I got to the bar fifteen minutes early and drank beer while I waited. When neither woman showed half an hour later I wondered if I'd got the right place. At ten to ten a young man strolled into the bar with a bag of newspapers. He made straight for me and said in English, 'Would you like a copy of the Paris *Evening News*? Five francs fifty, all written in Paris in English.'

I took out a ten-franc piece.

'There are plenty of people here. How did you know I'm English?'

He laughed. He was a thin, dirty-looking man in his mid-twenties, and he had a little beard which he held his hand up to when he laughed, covering his lips. As if he was saying something smutty.

'I just know.' He sniggered into his hand.

'How?'

'It's obvious.'

I looked around at the other people in the café. Maybe it was obvious. Most of them were younger than me, except one old couple who looked American in their tan shower-proof macs and their too-even teeth. The waiter stared back at me across the tiny wooden counter at the far end of the room. He knew I was English too. It's obvious.

'I even know your name,' said the newsvendor. 'You're Mr Jenner.'

'Bull's-eye, clever clogs. Sit down and have a beer.'

He shook his head.

'Not here, Mr Jenner. You follow me.'

'I rather expected to eat, you know? I've been here a long time.'

But I was speaking to his back. The newsvendor loped back out of the door. The waiter at the bar looked as if he rather expected me to eat, too. It was that kind of shoestring place. I waggled some bank notes at him and stood. The newsvendor stood outside the café, glowing regularly in a flashing orange light. He looked like an escapee from the beatnik days, a time-traveller. Or maybe from the late sixties, 'Ho ho ho Chi Minh.' The waiter took my money with bad grace. I went in pursuit of the newsvendor.

He strode off at a cracking pace, uphill and away from the bright lights. I followed about twenty paces behind and every time the newsvendor came to a corner he waited for me, just a few seconds, just so I didn't lose touch, then he was off again. We went down a long dark lane, just bigger than an alley. There was a tall wall on one side and unlit buildings facing the wall. Then we emerged into a bright street, not exactly a boulevard but a street with flashing neons and passing taxis and people strolling. The newsvendor went into a café and sat in a pool of yellow light. He lit a cigarette and drew in deeply.

I went in.

'Are you a drama student or something?'

He waved at the waiter. 'Two beers.' He held out his hand and smiled. 'I'm sorry. I'm Smith, believe it or not. Tom Smith.'

'American?'

'That's right. An American in Paris. Eleanor asked me to meet you in that bar. She said her meeting with... er, I don't remember the other person's name. Anyhow, she said their meeting was cancelled and she had to do something else so would I pick you up. So I did. I'm sorry it was late, but I had to do my paper round first.'

'What's your paper round?'

'The left-hand side of boulevard Saint-Michel from about half-way up, plus a couple of the streets behind.'

'You deliver all over there?'

'No. I sell them from café to café.' He smiled. 'For however much I can get. Are you shocked?'

'Disgusted. Where are we going?'

'Nowhere. She asked me to give you her address for tomorrow.'

He pushed a piece of paper over to me. 'It's outside Paris. You'll have to hire a car, I should think. Will you pay for our beers?'

'Of course... is this a game, Tom?'

He frowned. His dirty young face wrinkled.

'What makes you ask that?'

'Well, you come along to the bar I'm waiting in and ask me to follow you. Then you dash off so's I can hardly keep up. Then we sit in a different café which doesn't appear to have any advantages over the one we were in except it's in a less public place, I'm clearly *not* going to get any supper, and you start giving me magical mystery tours for outside Paris. "Is it a game?" is what I asked.'

He put some coins on the table.

'That'll pay for the drinks, Jenner. I gave you Eleanor's address because that's where it is. I don't know what I'm supposed to do about it. I didn't stop in the café you were sitting in because the owner doesn't like us newspaper sellers and certainly wouldn't let me sit down for a friendly drink with one of his customers. I asked would you pay for the drinks because you looked to me like you had more dough than me. I'll be seeing you.

57

He stood, scraping his chair. The waiter came for the money. Young couples stopped swapping sweet nothings over their red table tops and stared at us for a second.

'You can rent a car outside the Gare du Nord. Avis or something.' Tom Smith turned on his heel and walked out.

'Do you have any food?' I asked the waiter.

'Sond-*which, croque-monsieur.*'

'I'd better take a ham sond-*which* ... in fact, I'd better have two. And another beer, *s'il vous plaît.*'

'*Jambon?*'

'*Oui, jambon.*' Which was another twenty per cent of my French vocabulary used up.

A small, furtive-looking man came into the café. He brought across a document and showed it to me, then spoke quickly in French.

'I can't help, I'm afraid, sir. I only speak English.'

'This card was dropped by your friend, I believe, or you.' His English was slow and halting, but clear enough. The document was an identity card.

'Not me, I'm English. Nor him, he's American.'

'I'm sure it was his.'

'No. The name's wrong and the picture too.'

'Okay. It is not yours?'

I pulled my passport out. 'Not mine. Find a policeman, give it to him.'

'It is not from your friend?'

'No, of course not. It doesn't look like either of us.'

The small man was very dark for a European, with sallow skin and deep-brown eyes. He took my passport between the thumb and forefinger of his right hand and flipped the front page open, expertly. I didn't argue. He stared at the picture and my name for a second, then gave the passport back to me.

'Where is your friend from?'

'He's not my friend. He's from Paris, I think. But he's American.'

The small man waved the identity card backwards and forwards.

'So this is a mistake. I'm sorry. I will take it to a police station.'

I nodded that I agreed, yes a police station sounded just about right for both him and his document. The waiter brought my sandwiches over and the small man left. Some kids at the other end of the bar jeered when the door was safely closed behind him and the man was yards away. One came and sat by me.

'Trouble with the flics, eh?'

Very young, every inch the student. Dark hair and beautiful blue eyes. The sort of boy who should be a girl.

'Not trouble, I don't think. Why are they so nervous, I see machine-guns everywhere?'

'Di Nemico. Do you know of him?'

'Tell me.' I bit into a sandwich. It was made of bread you could break your teeth on. I chewed and it felt like rubble in my throat.

'An Italian big man. Somebody shot him near here. The police are going crazy. So they go crazy at us, they go crazy at you. What's your name, Englishman?'

'Dan Leno. I've got to go.'

I paid a fortune for the rubble sandwiches I hadn't eaten, then left. I began to walk down towards the river bank, where I knew I could get a taxi. It wasn't difficult to find. It's never uphill to a river.

Chapter Fifteen

I think my ex-wife must have been having a laugh at my expense, because the hotel she'd recommended to me was fifty yards from the place de la Bastille and on Saturday nights – which this was – every motorcycle owner in Paris drives round and round Bastille for a couple of hours, making sure their engines work and seeing how many coppers they can annoy by not wearing helmets. The answers are yes and quite a lot; I know, because I had the noisiest hotel room I've ever not slept in and at about two a.m. hundreds of Parisian policemen turned up with sirens and whistles and blue lights and everything and carted off as many as they could carry. By that time I was on my second night of not sleeping and I'd given up and sat on the balcony to watch the fun. It was too hot to sleep anyway.

*

Nine a.m. on the Sunday morning a very tired and bleary-eyed Jenner was picking his way breakfastless through the concrete jungle of a place called Saint-Denis, a suburb to the north of Paris and not the kind of place I expected to find there at all. I thought only England specialised in concrete walkways and ten-year-old slums. I was wrong; the Parisians had a slum building programme as big as anything we developed in London, and Saint-Denis is the fruit of the brave new French world. Eventually I found the doorstep I wanted and asked the young man who opened the door did he speak English. He was a burly, short man aged around twenty-five. He had a headful of thick curly hair and I hadn't caught him on his way out to mass because he was wearing a dirty T-shirt and faded jeans. No socks, no shoes. The young man ran his fingers through his hair and didn't even have to think whether he spoke English or not... he just said '*Non*'.

'Do you know Eleanor Wallace? Lenny Wallace?'

'*Non.*'

'So you don't know Juliette Saint-Croix, either?'

'*Non.*'

'Would you still not know her if I gave you fifty quid, sport?'

'*Non.*'

Not *possiblement non*, or *peut-être non*, just plain old *non*. No work even for *my* phrase-book there. He closed the door with no further ado. I turned my back on Mr Know-no-one's scratched-paint front door and leaned on the communal balcony railing. Paris was even hotter than London had been and a haze hung over the suburb already, even before half-nine. I looked down at the street. Five floors, plenty of car-parking and a little piece of tarmac kept free for topping yourself on when it all got too much. Go up another two floors, one last leap and splat... *confiture de fraises*. I could have been in Leeds or Glasgow or Bristol. I walked along the baking concrete balcony and down the stairs. The lift was broken and the stairs smelt as if a dog had died there. I could hear voices at the foot of the stairwell. Young men's voices. I went back to the scruffy door and knocked again.

'Look, pal,' I said, 'I know you don't want to talk to me and I don't really understand why. But take this...' I offered him my card with the name of the hotel I was staying at written on the back. I'd written it before I'd come, the plan being I'd shove the card through Lenny's door if I found no one there. Scruffy young Frenchmen with vocabularies restricted to '*non*' counted as 'no one there'.

'Take it.' I thrust the card into his hand and turned away. A young woman walked in the street below. From five floors up I had a foreshortened view of her, but she was blonde and she was young and she swung a nice leg as she climbed into a beaten-up 2CV. I think they must supply 2CVs from the factory like that. The girl was blonde okay and young, but it could have been anyone. Realistically it could have been anyone.

The curly-headed man had closed the door again while my back was turned. I returned to the smelly stairs. I passed two young men as I descended, obviously the voices I'd heard

61

earlier. They were dark-haired and sallow-skinned, dressed in lightweight suits. They looked out of place, resting on stinking suburban stairs. The young men were smooth and smart and expensive-looking. This place was mangy dogs chasing starving cats. It was dirt and ancient, rusted cars and unemployment. This wasn't the place for men in mohair and Ray-Bans and it wasn't the place for Eleanor. The young men saw my limp and they saw my walking-stick, so they deferred politely to me as I passed. I smiled and said thanks but they didn't speak. Maybe they were holding their breath against the stench of the stairway. When I reached the street about a hundred little heads were poking out of a hundred little windows above me. A kid had stuck gum on the door-handle of my rented Peugot, and by the time I'd cleared that off I felt as if I'd picked up a regular audience. 'Very good joke!' I called. They were too far up for me to know whether anyone was laughing or not. 'Very good joke. Bye-bye for now.' And I waved, 'Bye-bye.' I sat down in the car. And now someone had gone and moved the steering-wheel. I climbed out of the passenger door and went round to the driver's side. All the heads were sticking out still, now laughing. Clearly laughing. I'd cheered up their Sunday morning, anyway.

*

I found a roadside phone box a few miles further on and called Juliette Saint-Croix again.

'I seemed to miss you last night. In fact, I'm making a habit of seeming to miss people.'

'Our meeting was cancelled. Didn't you see Eleanor today at the flat?'

'No. I only got the man who don't speak English. My relationship with him is, uh...'

'The same man as you spoke to on the phone? Her boyfriend?'

'Well, Miss Saint-Croix, I don't know if he was her boyfriend or what. It's not easy, if one can't understand a word the other says. And for the same reason I don't know if he's the man I spoke to on the phone.'

'It would be him.'

'For a pretty girl with money, Eleanor has a weird taste in boyfriends, Miss Saint-Croix.'

'Maybe she does. Look, meet me at La Coupole at four. I'll see if I can't sort things out in between. I'm sorry you've been sent on a wild goose chase twice.'

'Where's La Coupole?'

'Montparnasse. Just ask any taxi driver for it.'

'Just ask any newsvendor for it . . . okay. But I hope this is going to be straightforward. I'm wasting a lot of time and other people's money here on something that should be straight-forward and isn't.'

But she'd gone.

*

Even though it was summer and a Sunday, Montparnasse was crowded and I couldn't find a parking space. I had to cruise the area and then I got lost and then I got on some one-way system and ended up fifteen minutes late, which I hate. I even hate thirty seconds late. It's supposed to be easier to park in Paris in the summer, according to my ex-wife's dud advice. She'd loaned me her map too.

La Coupole is a great barn of a place, more of an eating hall than a restaurant. There are hundreds of tables and quite a few stiff-looking waiters ready to frog-march you to the seat they reckon you should have (i.e., uglies and penniless at the back, big mouths and fancy dressers at the front). Just as I was being shown to the furthest corner I was bagged by a middle-aged woman in a broad-brimmed blue hat.

'You must be Jenner. I'm on the terrace.'

I followed her back to the terrace. She smiled and talked and talked, all at once. I just listened.

'They took you back there because you look so English, and the English have a reputation with Parisian waiters.'

We sat.

'What for?'

She smiled more broadly. 'Meanness.'

Juliette Saint-Croix was a young-looking late forties, I'd have guessed. She was small, about five-four, but not small for French women. She had a good figure and was very well dressed in a lightweight blue and white suit; her dark hair was cut by a good hairdresser and her fingers carried some baubles which certainly hadn't come from Woolworth's. Up-market; ooh, up-market. She ordered a beer for me and I said, 'I'm glad I found *someone*,

63

Miss Saint-Croix, because I was getting worried. I was beginning to feel like the man whose best friend wouldn't even tell him.'

'Tell him what?'

'Uh . . . why people will go out of their way to avoid him.'

'I'm sorry, Mr Jenner?'

'Jimmy, please.'

'Okay, Jimmy. I don't know why Eleanor is behaving so, so erratically. She's been doing it for some weeks.'

'Since Charlie's book was launched in London?'

'Since before, as he's no doubt told you.'

'Let me put my cards on the table. Charles Wallace has paid me to find his daughter. Now, he obviously doesn't expect me to come back with the girl under my arm. I think he'll be satisfied with a phone call and a little more of the old familial contact. That's all I'm trying to arrange. And to arrange it I would like to see the girl and talk to her and find out what's on her mind, which is not possible at present because she treats me as if I'm a writ-server chasing her all over Europe.'

'I'm sure she doesn't.'

'And I am sure, Miss Saint-Croix, that Eleanor Wallace has dug herself something of a hole. I don't care if she is pregnant, taking heroin, screwing a Catholic priest or all three, I don't care what the problem is. I want to *talk* to her. Please tell her that, will you?'

'*If* I see her.'

'You're not sure?'

Juliette Saint-Croix shook her head. White light bleached the street behind her while her face was in deep blue shadow from the hat.

'Only what you've been given. She's my friend's daughter. She contacts me when she wants to. I have no control over the girl . . . woman, now.'

She touched her hat and moved in her seat, so that a slash of light fell across her cheek. I gulped at my beer and waved for another.

'You're Charlie's friend?'

A laugh burst from her lips. It was loud enough that a copper standing near us on the pavement turned and stared at us.

'No, no! Good God no! One of that horror's friends?' She laughed again. 'I went to school with Eleanor's mother.'

'You don't like Charlie Wallace?'

'Does anyone? I told her not to marry him . . . in fact, I told her not to marry the one before and the one after. Angela – Eleanor's mother – is easily taken in by men. Anyone who looks artistic.'

'Does she have any contact with her daughter?'

'How can she from so far away?'

Quite.

*

We walked along the crowded street. People were taking their afternoon stroll. In England people stroll to work off their lunches. The French stroll to give their clothes an airing. Beautiful people walked along boulevard Montparnasse, it seemed like thousands of them. Beautifully dressed. I was glad I'd worn a suit. I'd have been okay in a morning coat and a topper. It's hard to overdress there.

'Do you have any plans, Jimmy?'

'I'll check and see what Charlie wants. It's his trip. You should tell her when you see her that he cares. You will see her?'

'I expect so. And you will, too. You have my address, so does she. Didn't she have a friend contact you last night?'

'Yes. An American.'

'Well ask him. Maybe she's with him.'

I thought of Tom Smith and his dirty face, his furtive look. 'I don't think so.'

We passed two more coppers. I said, 'Eleanor's friend said Paris was full of machine-gun police because of the Di Nemico business. The man who was shot.'

We had stopped next to a young North-African-looking woman selling flowers. She looked at me and smiled a gappy smile. She had a weather-beaten, tired face.

'English rose for the lady?' she said in English, pushing a foil-wrapped single rose at me. I wondered if I bought some Gitanes and walked around smoking them, if I bought a jacket two sizes too big and wore it with a shirt with no collar, if I kept a few high-roast coffee beans in my top pocket so I smelled of them all the time . . . I wonder if they'd still spot me on sight as an Englishman.

'No we don't want any bloody roses,' I said. 'Nor ferns, nor silver paper nor gappy smiles from you. Now sling your hook.

The North-African-looking woman kept smiling and kept holding out the rose. 'Rose, lady?'

'No,' said Juliette Saint-Croix. 'Paris is like that all the time. Always over-policed. Not especially now.'

I bought the rose. It cost two quid as well. I don't like French people thinking English people are mean, so I bought the rose and gave it to Juliette. What's two quid anyway?

'Can I have dinner with you?' I asked, determined to get my two quid's worth.

'No. I'm busy.'

'With Mr Saint-Croix?'

She smiled and squeezed my arm.

'There's no Mr Saint-Croix, nosy Mr Jenner. I'm sure she'll turn up. Don't worry.'

'I'm not worried. What do I have to worry about?'

'Eleanor. I can see you're worried.'

'It's just a job to me. I hardly know her.'

She gave me one of those knowing female looks.

'I'm not worried!' I repeated.

We were next to the stairs to a Métro station. She went down them without saying another word.

Chapter Sixteen

Paris ended not with a bang but a whimper. Charlie Wallace didn't answer his phone. About a million times he didn't answer his phone. By the next morning he still wasn't answering his phone, but Caroline Cholmondley-Smythe was and so was Charlie's agent (whose number Caroline gave me).

'Oh *yeah*, you won't get him now.'

'Thanks. Where is he?'

'Well, what's it about? I mean I'm his agent, you can deal with me.'

'It's personal.'

'I'd ring in two weeks, Mr what's-your-name.'

'Jenner.' Again. 'Two weeks is too long. I'm doing some work for him and I need to speak to him, okay? Now is when I need to speak, not two weeks.'

'What kind of work?'

'Just where is he?'

There was a pause in Shaftesbury Avenue, or wherever Charlie's English agent's office was. I could almost see young lovelies doing Miranda on the other side of his desk, voices low so's not to disturb the great man's telephone call. They would all want a part in *Cats* and were willing to demonstrate their ability by quoting at length from Shakespeare. Charlie's agent wouldn't even have a part in *Cats* to offer.

'Portugal. Southern Portugal. He's doing a part in an American soap.'

'In *Portugal?*'

'Mr Jenner baby, this is a very big soap. Megabucks, which is

67

the only reason I would advise a man like Charlie, a star, to do it. Everyone who's anyone does this soap.'

A star?

'Are you serious? Charlie Wallace is a star?'

'In America Charles Wallace is The English Gentleman. He'd be a natural for a part such as the one I'm describing which I shouldn't really be discussing. Call him in two weeks.'

'You don't have a number in Portugal?'

'None I'm giving out. Call him in two weeks or leave a message with us and we'll get back to you.'

'Don't bother. You realise I've been taping this conversation, don't you? And I'm going to play the tape back to your client when I see him.'

'I still can't help. Give me a message and I'll see he gets it.'

'Okay, the message is that Eleanor is avoiding me too and I'm coming home to England. He knows my number. Got it?'

'Got it. Did you really tape the conversation?'

I'm lying on my back in my room at the Hotel Berry. The smell is rising from the fish restaurant over the street. The traffic's going round and round Bastille, hot Bastille. The couple in the next room are bonking again and I say, 'Click. I've just turned the machine off now, Mr Mannystein. Click.'

'Mandlestein!'

Click. If you lean out of the window you can just see the great big place de la Bastille, which is nothing like Clissold Park. I have a plane to catch, and cannot spend my time hanging out of hotel windows.

Chapter Seventeen

George Tiler had a house in Wiltshire as well as the flat in Ratcliff. I went to Wiltshire to tell him about Gilligan. George had a garden party going, with lots of hooray Henrys sipping orange juice and Spanish champagne on his lawn. Leila was there, with her ancient Italian count called Paolo only she called him Pollo and he was kind enough to chuckle as if he'd never heard it before. 'Pollo is my chicken, Jimmy. And Jimmy is my Spade, Pollo. Ha ha ha ha.' What did I ever see in her? George guided me away from the Henrys and the spiked orange, through huge french windows into his drawing-room. The closed doors muffled the jollity on the lawn. Behind the glass was his view of his friends, then behind the friends a wild and uninterrupted vista to the Ridgeway, so that you'd hardly know there were manicured fields and well-trained cattle in hidden farming valleys between George's house and the ridge. The drawing-room was tasteful blue oil drag and books that looked unopened . . . ever. Behind the glass the countryside had something of the atmosphere of the room. Tidy, decorated. George poured me a Scotch and I sat and spoke.

'We met in a boozer in Islington. Near the antique market.'

'In the evening?'

'In the evening. He was with a friend, a black man aged, oh I don't know. Aged a muscular thirty.'

'Did the black man stay there the whole time?'

'He wasn't really the kind of fellow you'd show the door, George. I mean he was five-ten high and five-ten wide and he didn't talk a lot except to repeat something your friend Terence had said. You know, for emphasis.'

'So he witnessed your transactions?'

'Well what's to witness? You were Gilligan's old friend, this fellow's Gilligan's new friend. The black fellow had come to oversee the changeover. That's all.'

'Witness, more like. Maybe he'd come to take a good look at you. To keep an eye on you, Jimmy. Did you think of that?'

'Not even in a joke, George. Not even in a joke. You want to hear the rest? Keep quiet, then. (a) I hand Terence Gilligan your envelope containing more than one thousand pounds... I never counted it because that's between you and him. (b) I said, "Listen, Terence, I believe this is a one-off gesture owing to your present financial plight – though it's difficult to see a man in a £200 distressed-leather body-fit jerkin as being in any sort of financial plight... okay?" (c) I say, "But, Terence, little friend, I do not believe this gesture would ever be repeated no matter how crap your present financial plight becomes in the future. If the bottom of the used-car market falls out, do not come knocking on these doors for a second sub, because I do not believe it will come your way."

'"Do something rude with the used-car market, Jenner," says Gilligan. "Archimedes and me, we're buying a country cottage in Umbria and George's subvention will help just a little with the capital cost."

'"How will you live?" I asked, as if I cared.

'"Easy," he says, "Archimedes is a designer. He will design and I will paint."'

George seems to light up. 'Wonderful,' he said. 'Just right.'

'You think so? I was puzzled by this, George, and asked whether Archimedes was as experienced at designing as Terence was at painting, because if so they were going to starve and then they'd be back asking for another contribution from you, my client, which is grief I'm sure you'd prefer to avoid. I mean, if he'd said, "Me and Archimedes, we're going into the olive-growing business, at which Archimedes has many years of previous experience," I might have felt a little more at ease with it. Anyway "d" was, I asked for a receipt for the money. And they went all abusive on me.'

George just laughed.

'But I wasn't really serious. You never said "Get a receipt." Do you feel free of him now?'

'Absolutely. Free as a bird. Well done, Jimmy... well *done*.'

'Thank you. Now do you mind telling me why you gave him

the money? Did he witness you murdering someone?'

'No, no.' George laughed again. 'He was my *friend*, Jimmy. We were very close. And I knew he needed a stake. He'd already told me his father would give him some money to get him out of his hair.'

'*How* out of his hair? How was he in it?'

He threw the glass doors open. The hubbub of George's friends was clear now, and then the grinding of gears as a car drove along some hidden valley. An old Morris, by the gears. We stepped on to the lawn.

'A son like that is no advantage to a man plying a trade like Gilligan Pater's along the Romford Road. I'm sure his father would have staked him the cost of a hovel in Umbria. Our friend Pollo over there has just such a hovel in mind. I've given Leila Terence's number.'

'You've already talked to the father, haven't you?'

He smiled slyly. 'I've done what I can to help Terence.'

'You told the father, so it would bring a crisis about. When I saw him first Gilligan's father had no idea his son was one of your lot. It was *obvious* he didn't know. Between then and now someone's told the father, and that someone is you. Now the son's getting out because he has to. You forced him . . . why?'

George Tiler shook his head. 'I wouldn't put it like that. Not *forced*.'

'You set me up, you bastard. No wonder he hated me so much. Why? What's he got over you?'

'Nothing.'

'Balls, nothing. What is it?'

'Don't be so melodramatic. Here's someone you know. By the way, did you get the black man's name and address?'

'No. Just his name.'

'I bet you did, Jimmy.'

Leila threw an arm around my shoulder and held an orange drink up to my lips. 'Jimmy, have some Buck's.'

'I don't want to drink, thanks. I've got to drive back.'

George marched away to join Tony Frames-Pargeter and a lot of blue-suited senior citizens on his lawn. Louise Frames-Pargeter was the best-looking man there.

'What's *this* thrash in aid of, Leila? He keeps having parties.'

'Oh . . . I don't know. He just wanted to get some friends over.'

'Including you and your count? Come off it. How do you match in with the huntin', shootin' and drinkin' set?'

71

Leila's Italian count was deep in conversation with a woman who addressed him in a loud voice, as if he was deaf instead of foreign.

'He wants Paolo to do something for him,' Leila said. 'Paolo's very keen on doing people favours. George wants Paolo to arrange a house for some friends of his in Umbria.'

We walked away from the crowd and sat on a little wooden bench, white-painted, at the edge of the lawn.

'That fellow's old for you, Leila.'

'He's not very demanding. He's rich, too.'

'That's what George said. Does George want money from him?'

She waved at the house. 'Are you joking?'

Silly question.

'I've been retained by Charles Wallace to find his daughter. You remember Eleanor?'

'Of course. She introduced me to my Italian honey. Why do you have to find her? I can give you her address. She lives near rue Vaugirard, quite a long way out from the centre of Paris.'

'Is that the flat she owns?'

Leila nodded. 'Where else?'

'Her father says she's not staying there and hasn't done for a long time. And I had an address from someone else but she wasn't staying there, either. I had the strong impression she was avoiding me ... now why would she want to do that, Leila?'

She didn't answer. Instead she stood and waved at her count. 'Paolo. Come on. I want to introduce you.'

'You already have,' I said, but it didn't help. We had to go through it again. It wasn't yet two in the afternoon and Leila was looking seriously sloshed.

'Paolo, Jimmy here's an old friend of mine, and he's been trying to contact Eleanor Wallace. You know?'

Paolo smiled and nodded that he knew. He was a grey-haired, gaunt, cadaverous-looking man in his early sixties and all his movements were slow and deliberate. Paolo slowly and deliberately put his arm round Leila's shoulders and slowly and deliberately allowed his face to fall into a smile.

'Paolo Bianchi, enchanted, Mr Jimmy.'

'Jenner. Jimmy Jenner. Should I call you Count Something?'

'No. I'm not a real count. I bought a property at home and the title went with it.' He shrugged. 'Of course, calling me "count" is a joke of which my darling Leila here is very fond. And her friend Eleanor, too.'

'You know her?'

'Certainly, Mr Jenner. And I'm sure I can contact her for you. You should let me put you in touch. Do you have a card?'

I gave him my business card.

'Leave it with me.'

'Thank you. She's difficult to find.'

And he smiled slowly. 'Leave it with me.'

I walked down to George's gravelled car park. The old Italian stood with Leila on a little mound, a grassy hummock. They waved in a friendly way and so did I. George affected not to see me leaving.

Of course the Rover didn't start. After a while a young man came over and said, 'Mr Bianchi says would you like to be taken back to London in his car? I will drive you and come back again. Or you can stay for the rest of the party and come home with them later.'

'It's too much trouble,' I said.

'Mr Bianchi insists.'

He was a big dark-haired man with a flat-featured face and thin lips. He leaned in my window and blocked out the light.

'You're very kind. I'd like to go now if possible. I'll send someone for the car.'

The large young man opened the door for me. 'You'd better leave the keys in it.' Then he showed me over to a Mercedes 500. Paolo Bianchi and Leila were still standing arm-in-arm on the hummock, and they waved their free hands again. I waved back. The Mercedes started, no trouble. On the seat beside me was an Italian newspaper. It was more than a week out of date and had the picture of Di Nemico looking for his contact lens on the front page. His murder would be a big deal for Italians, of course, for weeks to come.

'Do you read Italian?' asked Bianchi's chauffeur.

'No. Just English and a bit of Spanish.'

'I'm sorry, all the papers we've got are Italian. My boss has them for the sports pages.'

'What sport's this fellow playing?'

I held up the photograph of Di Nemico so he could see it in the mirror.

The chauffeur smiled. 'I'll put the radio on. It'll only take an

73

hour to London. Maybe an hour and a half to Stoke Newington.'

At the gate to George's drive was a car with a couple of men in it. Old George certainly liked to have bouncers at his parties. The chauffeur nodded to them. I flipped the pages of the Italian newspaper aimlessly. The leather seat of the Mercedes pressed into my back and we accelerated towards London.

Chapter Eighteen

There were tape messages for me when I arrived home. I ignored them and rang Little Leon, a very small black retired car thief, aged twenty-five. Leon now mends cars instead of stealing them, which must make him one of HM Prison Service's few successes. I asked him to fetch and fix the Rover.

'Where is she, Jim-boy?'

'Wiltshire.' I read him George Tiler's Wiltshire address.

'Where's that at? It's outside London, right?'

'That's right, Leon.'

There was a long silence, then he said, 'M3 motorway, right?'

'M4, Junction 13, spa?'

'I'm on it, Jim-boy. I have the tow-truck keys in my hand.'

'Leon – cheap, okay?'

'I hear you. You should have a Mini or a 2CV if you wants cheap.'

'Also please don't call me "Jim-boy."'

He laughed and put the phone down.

I made coffee and played the messages. Only one was interesting.

'It's me. I'm sorry I missed you. I didn't want to. Quite the opposite, in fact. I came to your hotel but you'd gone. I really didn't miss you on purpose. I do desperately want to talk. I want to talk to someone, Jimmy. Please can we meet? I can't leave here at the moment, but if you could be at the Hotel Berry tomorrow afternoon, I'll come and explain everything to you. Please come if you can. I'm sorry to have given you a runaround. Please come.'

I rang the hotel and made a booking. If I'd known a policeman would be sitting next to the reception clerk reading the register even as I rang I might have thought it a bit odd. Policemen don't go round reading hotel registers much in England . . . but then they were looking for a suspected murderer in Paris. The copper must have thought it was his birthday when the suspect rang and made a booking for another night's stay. All he had to do was call his boss, station a few boys in blue round the hotel and wait for big bad Jenner to walk in and get himself arrested. He'd be getting commendations, police medals and promotions. I'd be getting caught.

Then I rang a travel agent and booked a flight to Paris, again.

'Paris again,' said the girl on the other end of the phone. She was the same one who'd made my first booking. 'We are having fun, Mr Jenner, aren't we? Paris *again*. Oh I *wish* it was me.'

'It's business.'

'But Paris is fun even for business. I *love* Paris.'

'Why-oh-why do I love Paris?' I sang and she giggled. It doesn't take much to amuse some people.

Chapter Nineteen

The mortuary door opened and a uniformed policeman came in. He was a high-ranker of some description. I sat on the wooden chair and told Letellier and his fat colleague everything I knew about the young man, and it wasn't much and it didn't take long. I told them I was looking for the daughter of a client. An English client. I'd gone to visit the flat in Saint-Denis because that was the address I was given where the girl might be.

'What's the girl's name?' asked Letellier.

'Don't you know? I was given to believe she was that young man's girlfriend. That's why I went to his flat.'

'What name did you have?'

'No name. Just the boyfriend's flat.'

'What was the girl's name?'

'Er . . . I think I have to treat that as privileged, Mr Letellier.'

The fat detective spoke to Letellier, who was obviously explaining what I meant by my last sentence.

'Not here,' said Letellier. 'No privilege here for you, Mr Jenner.'

'Then I'd better see a lawyer.'

'Lock him up,' said the fat detective in English. 'Lock him up and leave him for a few days. One week. We'll ask again in one week.'

'Eleanor Wallace is the name. She fell out with her father.'

Well, I don't know whether they could do it or not. I wasn't going to spend a week in the slammer in France for Eleanor Wallace nor anyone else. No hundred quid a day is worth that.

'She ran away from him. Recently he became concerned for

77

her well-being and asked me to come here and see if I couldn't find her. Find out how her circumstances were. I suppose he wants me to heal their argument and bring her home.'

'Spell the name,' said Letellier. I did. The uniformed policeman took a note of it and left.

'Why did this father ask you to find the daughter?'

'That's not for me to question. It seemed at the time to be a straight-forward request to make of an English private detective. Isn't it here?'

The short fat policeman grunted and flapped his coat again. He went to the drawer with the corpse in it and stared at its face. Letellier stared at his fingernails, as if his colleague was embarrassing him. 'I'll ask the questions,' he said. 'When did you last see this man here alive?'

'About nine a.m. last Sunday morning. That's when I left him.'

'What did you talk about?'

'*Nothing*. He didn't speak English.'

The short man looked up from the drawer. 'Are you sure?' he asked.

'I'm sure.'

He frowned. 'Positive?'

'Positive. That man didn't understand a word I was saying. Is there some reason for thinking I'm wrong?'

'He could have been . . . acting.'

'No.'

'And he was in good health when you left him at nine last Sunday?'

'Well, I'm no doctor, you know? But he was a bloody lot better-looking than that.'

The short man closed the drawer with an angry slam. The sound echoed round the empty, neon-lit room. There was a silence, then I became aware of the sound of an air-conditioner. There were murmured voices outside the room, too.

'Thank you for your opinion,' said Letellier. 'Tell us what passed between you, please?'

'I asked did he know Eleanor Wallace, he didn't understand. I asked had he ever heard of Eleanor Wallace. He didn't understand. I offered him my card and wrote the name and address of the Hotel Berry on the back just in case he did know Eleanor but simply couldn't understand English. He took the card and slammed the door on me. Now you ask how well I knew him because you've found my card on his body. I'm telling you, mister... *that's* how well I knew him. I don't even know his name.'

'Could there have been anyone inside the apartment?'

'Possible. Of course it's possible. Didn't look like it but he could have had the Household Cavalry in his front room and I wouldn't have known. 'Course, they'd have had to have been keeping quiet. But he *could* have done.'

'Was he frightened? Could someone have frightened him?'

'Not me or my client, y'know? And I don't know whether someone else did.'

'He didn't give you an idea he was frightened?'

'I don't know! He didn't speak English... how many times?'

The short policeman said something to Letellier, then went outside and brought in two white-coated morticians. They were big beefy fellows, like dockside labourers or men from a road gang. The short policeman pointed at the drawer and they opened it and began to lift the curly-headed corpse out.

'Who did you see while you were there?' asked Letellier.

'No one.'

'You didn't pass anyone on the street? There was no one standing by his door?'

'Yes, a couple of smartly dressed youths on the stairwell.'

Letellier said something to the short detective and motioned with his hand in a spiral, indicating a stairwell. The morticians dumped the curly-headed corpse on one of the big clean tables. The sheet was still over it.

'Describe them.'

'Young. Flashy, very smart clothes, expensive dark glasses. They wore perfume.'

'Age?'

'Early twenties. Dark-haired. Latin-types...' I allowed myself a smile. 'I would have thought French.'

'No one in yellow clothes?'

'Yellow clothes?'

'The sort an Indian would wear. An Asian, I mean. Like a... like a sheet wrapped around them.' Letellier twirled his hands around his body to indicate how the sheet would wrap. He looked like an exotic dancer.

I shook my head.

'I mean white people in yellow Indian clothes who spoke English. People heard them.'

79

'Not me.'

'People heard them. People heard him scream, too.'

'I didn't. He didn't scream or anything while I was there and there were no mateys in yellow clothes, all right. I'd have noticed them.'

'Let me explain our problem,' said the short policeman suddenly, and he twirled the nylon sheet away from the corpse's feet like a magician. The two morticians were his magician's assistants, standing with impassive faces and folded bare arms. The lifted sheet revealed a very bloody pair of feet, pulpy purple with red flesh. 'Come closer and see. We think this was done with a...'

'Hammer.' Letellier supplied the word.

'We think it was done with a hammer and we think it was done by Englishmen. We *know* it was done before nine-twenty on Sunday morning because that's when his body was discovered. He was on the ground below his apartment. The only identification we found on his body was your card, Mr Jenner. We have a report of an argument coming from the house. It was in English. We have a report of screams.' He pointed at the feet again. 'Not surprising. We know two Englishmen dressed in yellow were looking for the apartment because they asked people. Englishmen are rare in Saint-Denis, if they were looking for apartments or driving hire cars. You understand what I mean?'

'You don't think I did this?' I said.

Letellier shrugged.

'How did he get the smashed forehead?'

'He was pushed or fell from his apartment. I think he was pushed, don't you?'

I tapped my leg and stood. 'You don't have a case against me. I couldn't lift that man and throw him over the parapet. Why don't you look for the Latin types I described? Or the Englishmen in Indian clothes?'

The short detective laughed loudly. 'Perhaps you are their confederate!'

The door opened and the high-ranking uniformed man came back. He was pinch-faced with dark, intelligent eyes. The eyes looked me over then he began to speak quietly in French. The short man frowned as he listened, clenching his fists and leaning his knuckles against the mica table top. After a few sentences the three policemen went into a huddle in the furthest corner of the room. They seemed to have forgotten me. I was left to make chapels of my fingers and stare at the ceiling. The morticians stood before me, a couple of hearth dogs. Men of stone.

'Great weather, eh?'

Nothing.

'I suppose you're a bit more used to it round here. It's rare for the likes of me, you know? Round our way it sloshes down all the time ... nice bit of hot weather like this is a godsend. A pal of mine was only saying the other day, it's a surprise Englishmen aren't born in wellington boots. Galoshes, rather.'

Nothing. I suppose mentioning Wellington wasn't all that tactful.

I lifted the plastic sheet to look at the feet again. Some plates, all blood and swelling. He was never going to wear size-nine dancing pumps again. Nor size-fifteen wellington boots even. *Galoshes*. I lifted a foot and looked over the damage. Most of the contusions were on the upper left side, that is my left as I looked at it. None underneath, few on the right side and none of those serious. They'd all definitely been made with a hammer. I stared at the blue-black feet, blue-black bruise. Blue-white dead-young-man skin. I wondered what he'd known that had been so important. Had he told it? I couldn't believe it was possible he hadn't when someone was bashing his tootsies with a ball-peen hammer. What could he have known? I dropped the sheet. The mistake we sometimes make is to think there's some logical reason for everything. Maybe someone beat him because he simply wanted to hurt. Maybe the dead man knew nothing except his feet hurt. Then his headache cured all that.

The conference broke up. The short detective and the uniformed copper left. Their feet squeaked on the linoleum outside. Not far, not many squeaks. Then there were quiet voices.

The silence was long enough for me to notice an electric hum, probably the refrigeration unit. From a room along the corridor the fat detective's voice came, raised and angry, rattling around the empty spaces between us, shaking the frosted glass in the door. A one-sided argument with a telephone. Letellier stared at me while I listened. I didn't understand a word, but I tried to look intelligent.

'Trouble?'

He shrugged but didn't speak. I tried again. 'What's he called, your colleague?'

'Meyer.'

'Peculiar name for a Frenchman, isn't it?'

'It depends where you're from. He's from the Saar.'

Letellier paused for a moment, staring at the dead man on the mica table top, then suddenly said 'Enough' in English and waved for the mortuary assistants to put the corpse back in his drawer. They tried but they took hold of him awkwardly. The plastic cover slipped to the floor. The mortuary men grunted and heaved. The corpse wigwagged his stiff arms and belched loudly. He didn't want to go back in that drawer and he didn't care who knew it.

'Were you ever a real policeman?' Letellier asked. The mortuary men were still fighting and dancing with the dead man.

'Oh yes. For some years.'

'But not a detective, I think?'

'You think right. I was a uniform policeman. I donated the lower part of this leg to policing the streets of London. Also I don't hear too well in this ear... I call it my interrogation ear. Yeah, I was definitely a policeman once... were you?'

But Letellier stared through me. He wanted to talk, not listen. He gave no sign of having understood. Something had changed his mood. I don't know what. Something he'd heard in his colleague's one-sided telephone conversation. Something the uniformed cop had said.

'Then you know. You know the work has...' He shook his head, as if the word had escaped him. He nodded at the two struggling men. The corpse wobbled drunkenly between them, laying its smashed head against the shoulder of one man while the other struggled with its feet.

'A comical side? It's always the same when things are so awful. They get funny, eh? What you need is a gurney.'

'What's a gurney?'

'A trolley for moving them about on. You can't tell me these men spend their lives heaving corpses backwards and forwards like this? What happens when they get a really fat one?'

Letellier pursed his lips and waited while the grunting and scuffling was going on. Then the white-coated men slammed the drawer shut. I wouldn't have been surprised if they'd locked it. A smear of blood remained on the mica table top, another on a mortician's smock.

'No,' said Letellier. 'Not funny. Sad. Take this man. This

man has a short life, I don't believe over thirty years. He has it ended by torturers, murderers. Then comes the investigation. Then come the police. We see sad things.'

He meant it.

'Do you know who he is?' I asked.

Letellier looked at me. 'Don't you?'

I shook my head. 'You don't think I was involved in this?'

'I don't know. It would be better if you were not.'

'If "better" is all you're concerned with, mate, it would be "better" if nobody had done it. I told you the truth. Why don't you go and look for the Latin types? Didn't anyone else notice them?'

He didn't reply. There was no chance to. Meyer burst back into the room. He shoved the black plastic bag bearing my belongings into my hand and said, 'What is you baggage?' Pronouncing it 'bagg-arshe'.

'A small Samsonite grip.'

'*Where*,' said Letellier. He pointed at the black plastic bag. 'That's all, yes?'

'I hope so.'

Meyer said, 'You will go with Letellier. With you bagg-arshe. You will take the night train from the Gare du Nord to England, via Dunkerque. Letellier will accompany you. He will make sure you get the train, do you understand?'

The short fat detective was angry and he didn't feel like hiding it. He had grey, bristly hair cut short, *coiffure* circa 1950. He had sharp piggy eyes and more than one chin. The piggy eyes glared and one of the chins had set, so that he spoke as if he was clenching his teeth between the words, biting off the last English consonant. I smiled patiently at the piggy eyes and shook my head slowly.

'I have a coupon for a return air ticket. I haven't even begun to think about my flight yet, let alone made a booking.'

Letellier raised his eyes to the ceiling. Meyer took hold of my elbow. It hurt.

'Monsieur Jenner . . . you will take that train and you are lucky not to face a magistrate in the morning with a charge of murder, or accomplice or something, anyway. Do you understand?'

'I don't really see the point of this. Either you think I didn't do it or you think I did. Either way, what . . .'

'You will go now. Letellier will take you.'

Meyer turned and strode away. From the far end of the room he aimed a burst of rapid French at Letellier, then clicked his fingers and his echoing, shower-room voice said, 'Let's go, okay?' Again.

I gave Letellier the black plastic bag and we left.

Part Two
Pass the Parcel

Chapter Twenty

I was in a dark garage. I'd come from the summer-night street and I'd passed through a small door into what seemed like complete darkness. I was in a garage in Chelsea, and the street outside led down to the traffic of the Embankment. The traffic roared, even at night, and the dull sound reached me even here in the garage, behind the closed door.

I leaned back against the door for the moment, to give my eyes a chance to get used to the darkness. The garage was very tall, maybe twelve feet high. It was 1930s, nearly mock-Tudor; a half-timbered structure built on the side of a Chelsea 'cottage'. The entrance to the garage was made of two big doors, cedarwood or the like. There was a postern set into the left-hand door and it was through this postern I had come, this postern which was behind my back now. I was still for a long time, longer than I'd intended. Then I could see better. I wasn't in the dark at all. Tiny shafts of street lighting penetrated the doors, slanting through the spaces between the doors and the jambs. I could see a car before me. A Mercedes 500. There were gardening tools and deckchairs hung on the wall beside the car. I could feel dirt and grit and concrete dust under my feet. I turned and moved slowly down the side of the Merc. I felt its paintwork under my hand; thick and creamy, cool after the stifling air that surrounded me. I peered into the gloom at the back of the garage. Nothing. I crouched and slipped a package from my pocket. I felt amongst the dirt under the Merc's rear wing, by the petrol tank. I cleaned some dirt off, then pushed the package in there. I stood and moved back towards the postern. I could smell perfume. Then an interior door opened behind me and a light clicked on. I turned. It was a young man, dark, small, slim. He wore an expensive suit. He clicked off the light again and spoke in the darkness.

'Don't move.'

I eased myself back towards the door and he said again, 'Don't move. I mean it.' Then, after a pause, 'I have a gun. I will shoot you. It's as simple as that. Just don't move.'

'I wasn't . . .'

'Keep still. I'll shoot you. Keep still.'

I kept still. The young man, I felt sure, was one of the boys I'd seen on my way down from the flat in Saint-Denis. He had a strong accent too. French, Italian. Something.

'I'm okay, sport. I'm staying still. Who are you?'

'Shut up.'

'Well look, I'm sure we can straighten this out. I mean, I came in here as a passer-by looking for a stray moggy, and I have a couple of friends waiting for me outside, so I'd better go out again now or they're going to miss me.'

We stood silent in the darkness for a few seconds.

'I mean, I don't know about all this guns business, cock. I'm just an innocent bystander who happened to stray on to your property. Why don't I just leave and we'll call it quits?'

And he said, 'Nowhere. You're going nowhere.'

He was right too. There was the faintest of clicks from the postern behind me, then one of the mock-Tudor half-timbers must have detached itself from the wall and fallen on me. I felt the cool metal of the Merc touch my cheek, just for a second, then there was the taste of the concrete floor on my lips. My mind felt dull, a rice-pudding needing a stir. There were the voices of two men and I couldn't understand what the voices were saying. Definitely two men and definitely I couldn't understand them. The concrete tasted salty. Now a third man's voice, raised and angry. A tiny slit of sodium light leaked under the cedarwood doors. Then it was truly dark and there were just the sounds of the men's voices turning in my head, turning, turning. Voices on their own. Turn as they would, I still couldn't figure out what they were saying.

Then it didn't matter. The perfume did and the salt did. The perfume mattered more than the voices and I was at the bottom of a deep stairwell. Faces looked over the banisters at me, first two, then one face. She had perfume too, but hers was different. Dark.

Chapter Twenty-one

When we left Meyer and his morgue Letellier didn't speak much. He confined himself to comments of the 'You buy your ticket here' and 'Make sure you have your passport' variety. If he wanted to talk, he didn't. He never left my side, though, until the train was rolling towards Dunkirk. He sat me in a huge first-class compartment, half a carriage long, and though there were few enough passengers the neat-minded booking clerk had seated us all together. I was opposite a small, dark-haired, American-looking girl. Letellier put my little bag on the rack above the girl and then went and leaned across the open doorway, as if to stop me making a run for it.

The dark-haired girl volunteered her name as Mandy. She was doing Europe on twenty dollars a day and she had a first-class Eurorail pass hung on a cord around her neck; a pass bought, I guessed, by her mother in Illinois. Why else have a first-class ticket but no money?

'How much is twenty dollars in pounds?'

'About twelve, I think,' said Mandy.

'I hope you have a nice time.'

She'd been to seven countries on that twenty dollars a day, which would have made anyone glum. Mandy simply looked dulled by it. 'Thank you,' she said. 'You too. And your friend.' She indicated Letellier at the end of the gangway.

'Oh him.'

But she'd turned her dull grey eyes to stare at our reflections in the train window. After a while Mandy opened a novel. Letellier leaned across his doorway, looking more than a little impatient. After a few awkward minutes there was a 'clonk' and the wheels began to turn. Letellier went out to the corridor between the coaches. I got there in time to see him skipping off the train, letting the door swing wildly behind him. Then the door's catch snapped shut. Letellier didn't look back. I leaned out of the window to see. The tracks and the platform of the Gare du Nord receded and so did Letellier's figure. The shapes lost definition and the white lights of the station withdrew too. I was surrounded by rushing darkness and high walls. Electric cables twanged above my head, the wheels rumbled and screeched below me. People watched TV in blocks of flats rising above the tracks. The TV screens threw coloured lights that fidgeted across the windows as our train passed. The heat beat down on Paris, even at night; sickening thick heat. I pulled the window up and went inside. At the far end of the carriage a young man stood by the door. He was tall and dark with casual clothes, a neat moustache, a jacket that was too big for him and a serious look on his face. The jacket left plenty of space round his armpit for his wallet, badge, gun and spare kepi. The young man ostentatiously avoided seeing me.

I sat. Mandy closed her novel and told me she came from a suburb of Quebec, not Wisconsin, North Dakota, Michigan or any of the other places those worthy American girls come from. She asked for the best place in London to eat and showed me a book on the subject which, judging by the prices quoted, had been researched in 1958.

'With twelve quid a day, you should stay at the YWCA and eat in your room. Buy sliced bread, ham and jam from a supermarket. Only take one bus ride a day and never under any circumstances get in a taxi.'

'Oh. That bad?'

'That bad, miss. No hamburgers or any of that stuff. If it rains remember the public libraries are free.'

The young Frenchman with the moustache was still there, still not noticing me. Letellier and Meyer certainly wanted to make sure I got out of France before I fell into the hands of one of them *juges d'instruction*. I closed my eyes and relaxed as best I could. The train was smooth enough but I was tense. Then the waiter came round with lukewarm coffee and stale rolls. Mandy took the opportunity to tell me about the development of the *grands boulevards*, which were built before Quebec had any suburbs for her to come from. That really surprised her. She'd stayed on one, too. Kellerman. Boulevard Kellerman. Another fellow with an unlikely German name . . . this one had risen to be a marshal of France. I never used to believe my teacher when he said that all the time we spent doing French history would have a use some day. It had seemed unlikely at the time. Mandy asked should we see each other in London. I told her I didn't expect we would.

I parted company with Mandy in the passport queue at Dover. Last I saw she was in the queue for EEC nationals, which was going to mean delay for her and probably no little confusion. How could she be so stupid as to go through the wrong channel when it was so clearly marked? I could have gone back to help but was feeling a little self-obsessed. At least she didn't have a ton of bagg-arshe like most of those kids touring Europe.

I walked out of the ferry terminal and ignored the bus laid on for the station. I didn't get the first train I could and I didn't want to. Instead I walked along the sea front in the early dawn light, watching the deep crimson disc of sunlight drag itself out of the Channel and wondering what the hell had been said to Letellier and his boss. Why does the sun look so close in the mornings? It can only be an illusion. Why such a dark red? Did the cops know Eleanor was in that hotel or not? Where was she now? In Paris or London? Drinking coffee with Auntie Juliette at the Coupole? Another bloody illusion.

Some disoriented crows marched along the beach like a skirmishing line of soldiers. Red sunlight glanced off their smooth black feathers while their scaly feet splashed in pools of blood-red water. Seagulls squawked jealous anger from the sky above. I was going to submit my account to Charles Wallace, okay, because finding Eleanor was the least of this. He could have done it himself if *finding* her was all he wanted. I leaned against the chipped and rusted blue-painted rail of the promenade and considered this problem until the sun was up properly and the crows had gone back to their motorways and fields. My eyes were sore and my neck ached. My leg ached too. I was acutely aware I could have been watching the dawn from a French police cell. I turned away from the beach and the Channel and France and went in search of a decent cup of coffee. I didn't find one. I was on the wrong side of the Channel.

When I finally made it to the station Mandy was still there. She had missed a couple of trains. I waited in the lavatory for the train so I didn't have to talk. It stank.

Chapter Twenty-two

I made it back to Stoke Newington in the late afternoon. It's only one train and one bus from Dover, but those last legs of journeys seem to take for ever. I dumped 'what is your luggage' in the hallway and flopped into a chair to read two circulars and a phone bill. This number at the bottom surely couldn't be pounds? Seems like every time I go away for a couple of days people come round and stuff demands for money through my letter-box. I'm frightened to leave the house.

I turned the answering machine on to see if all this money I was paying actually bought me any service. There was a message from George Tiler, one from my ex-wife and one from a woman in Northampton. She wanted her husband found, but quickly. I ran a bath and played the tapes again.

Beep. 'Call me as soon as you get home, will you, Jimmy? I think we are at last about to see some of the cash from the place in Cristo.'

My ex-wife about our place in Spain.

Beep. 'George here, Jimmy. Call me when you can, as soon as? I need . . .'

I ran from the bathroom and fast-forwarded him. He needs, he *needs* . . . he needs a nanny. Then there was the long rambling message from the woman in Northampton, one Mavis Lasker. Mavis's husband had disappeared in London. Poor her, no luck for Mavis. Her husband had run off and there she was, the only woman in England under sixty called Mavis. After the bath I rang her. I told her – yelling over the background voices of her kids – that it's expensive to use someone like me to find her

92

husband. Had she tried the police? Yes. Salvation Army? Yes. Was she claiming dole? Because if she was the DHSS would want to find Ronald Lasker and make him cough up his share of supporting his family. They could find him if they wanted to and it wouldn't have to cost her a bean.

'Do you think, Mr Jenner?'

'I'm sure they can if they want to. Press them. Tell them it could save them money. They'll like that.'

She said she would press them and then she'd get back to me if it didn't work, which wasn't exactly what I'd had in mind. The husband had come down here looking for work, too. He'd found something, whatever it was.

I rang my ex-wife and we discussed how our Spanish lawyer had told her that one of us had to go to Spain to swear in front of a magistrate before we could recover our property and the cash value thereof. I am *persona non grata* in Spain owing to me hijacking a couple of English criminals there some years ago and I did not fancy the trip.

'They'll arrest me, Judy,' I said.

Well, it wasn't so much the hijacking of the criminals as the fact that one died en route which has upset the Spaniards so.

'I don't think so now, Jimmy. He says it's okay now.'

'I don't want to find out. It's not him they'll arrest.'

'Just share the journey through France with me. Drive with me to Biarritz. Wait for me a couple of days while I go and swear this thing, sign the documents on the property sale and then we could have a short break together and celebrate.'

I thought the whole point of divorce was to take a long break apart and celebrate. I didn't say so.

'Why not fly?'

'That was not the right answer, Jimmy. The right answer is "Yes dear, I'd love to go to Biarritz with you".'

'I can't actually drive across France at the moment, Judy.'
'Why?'

She wasn't very amused when I told her why. She seemed to think I was doing it on purpose.

'We could fly to Gibraltar,' I suggested. I didn't mean it, of course.

'I'll fix it. I'll phone you. Bye bye, Jimmy. Lots of love.'

Coo coo, lovely dove. What's she feeling guilty about? I switched the phone machine on again and took my bath. As I slipped into the hot water I knew the day was a write-off. I needed sleep. I woke in the early evening, stiff and chilled in my cold bathwater. The phone was ringing. *That's* what we pay them for. The tape cut in, first my voice, then Charlie Wallace's. I stood, grabbed a towel and walked, dripping wet, into the living-room. He hung up before I reached the phone.

Chapter Twenty-three

'Sorry, I rather feel as if I dropped you in it.' Cool as you like. Charlie Wallace's voice on the phone, late at night on a dark, thick summer's evening.

'*No?*'

'I do. I know you'll argue and I'm sorry but I do. It was all a case of mistaken identity, the French cops say. I've been there. I just missed you, otherwise I would've sorted it out.'

'Been where?'

'Paris.'

'Where are you now?'

'London.'

'See her?'

'No. I didn't actually *see* her. I went to see Juliette Saint-Croix. And Eleanor rang her while I was there and spoke to me. You did a good job, Jimmy, I'm grateful.'

'You could have spoken to her on the phone from here. You could have done it without leaving Portugal, Charlie. If you wanted to play daddikins you could have done it long distance.'

'I wanted to *see* her.'

'But you *didn't*. Are you really making an advertisement in Portugal?'

'*Advertisement?*'

'For soap. Your agent said you were doing some soap advertisement. I said that wouldn't wash.'

'Very funny.'

'Do the French cops know where your daughter is?'

On my lap was a newspaper and on the third page was a little headline, one of the ones they put on top of two-paragraph reports – 'Di Nemico: Man Found Dead'. The article claimed that by a mixture of perspicacity and diligence the French cops had tracked down one gang member from the guys who'd shot the Italian. He'd been found in the suburb of Saint-Denis. I could see Letellier and Meyer striking diligent and perspicacious poses. No doubt within a day or two they'd let it slip that the man they'd found dead was young, of Mediterranean origin and had fallen from a great height after arguing with his confederates in crime. Policemen all over the world are just too devious for anybody's good. I flapped the newspaper at a fly.

'The French cops seem to have all the answers, Charlie,' I said when he didn't reply. 'Maybe they know what took you to Paris. So far I'm confused about why you sent me there, leave alone why you went there. I expect this has a lot to do with your daughter's dead boyfriend. Why don't you fill me in?'

'I can't. I don't know anything to fill you in about. And my daughter doesn't have any dead boyfriends.'

'Have you seen the evening paper? The *Standard*'s Paris correspondent has been fed a line by the French cops that your daughter's dead boyfriend shot this Di Nemico character.'

'Bull.'

'It's true.'

I read him the article.

'It doesn't say that. It doesn't associate this man with my daughter. You're a mischievous man, Jenner. My daughter is an innocent young victim of circumstances. Because of her being inadvertently at the same address as this man.'

'So she knew him?'

He said nothing. My window was open and two girls stood under a streetlamp, now puffing cigarettes, now swaying to their ghetto-blaster. They held the cigarettes with a grand air, surely something they'd rehearsed. They swayed unselfconsciously, though.

'We have to meet, Charlie,' I said. 'I've still got a load of your money.'

'Keep it.'

'You can't be serious?'

But Charlie was. He said he'd decided I should keep it as a bonus, owing to my having done such a good job, splendid and discreet it was, at such short notice. Having his daughter phone him.

96

'I didn't. You and Juliette did that. I've just been backwards and forwards about a million times on planes and trains, recognising bodies and the like. Turn it up, Charlie.'

'Keep the money. No problem. Keep it . . . I want you to. Think of it as a continued payment for the exercise of your discretion in the future.'

Charlie hadn't had much practice at being tactful.

'I'm not a Turkish railway guard or something, you know? Cut the discretion rubbish. I'll bring your money round in an hour.'

'Not now,' he said quickly. 'I'm going out.'

'Tomorrow then.'

'Tomorrow I have appointments. And the day after I have to go to Portugal to finish my "soap" character part. And after that I have to unavoidably go to New York. It's a dog's life, my game . . .'

Outside the girls had stopped swaying and turned their ghetto-blaster right up. A young boy had joined them and sat back on the wall with them. The boy wore a beanie and was talking earnestly with the girls. I closed the window to muffle the noise from the kids' machine. Charlie was still talking about how tough an actor's life is.

'. . . and a gorgeous blonde secretary with tits like brass torpedoes out to about here. But what's that to you, eh? Bugger all, that's what it is to you. Listen, if you really won't keep this money. If you really won't keep it, well I don't know. If you won't keep it send a cheque to this address. But really you should keep it. I owe you a lot, James. I know I can rely on someone like you.'

'Do you really have a gorgeous blonde secretary?'

'No. That's just it. I had one while I was writing *In the Can.*'

'What's that?'

'I *gave* you one! My book that takes the lid off Hollywood. Everyone thinks the title refers to filming, but it really refers to canned sardines . . . get it?'

'Tell me.'

'They are oily and jammed in close together, there are too many of them and they stink.'

'Charlie, there are matters we have to discuss. Missing persons, mistaken identities, all that caper. Dead terrorists in newspapers, do you get my drift?'

'I don't know a thing about dead terrorists in newspapers and neither does Eleanor.'

'You're telling me that Eleanor's boyfriend getting killed and her disappearing is just a coincidence? You're telling me that the boyfriend getting himself under suspicion for shooting an Italian politician and then him dying and the French police arresting me, those are all coincidences too?'

'Juliette gave you the wrong address, Jimmy. That place was a squat of some sort Eleanor had stayed in months ago, before she even met you, I think. And the bloke who lives – *lived* there, had no contact with Eleanor. Juliette Saint-Croix never got anything exactly right in her life. Once the police checked they realised you'd simply gone to the wrong house and given the bloke your business card, so they let you go.'

'The man in the mortuary was the man I saw at your daughter's old flat, right?'

'Right.'

'Well, no one had made any mistake about him, Charlie. He was dead, you know? And now he's turned up in the paper as an assassin.'

'It appears.'

'And during this same period your daughter did a runner from life in general and you in particular. No one could find her, right?'

'Right.'

'Good. I'm glad we've got that far. The man in the mortuary wasn't about to commit anything to paper, but there were definite signs that the poor fellow had been tortured, okay. And my bet is they weren't torturing him so they could get the address of his bookmaker or have him stand on the table and recite Baudelaire. I mean, the people who did that to Eleanor's boyfriend really wanted something. And if they didn't, if it was a mix-up, my bet is these people will want to correct their mix-up, and I do not mean by giving him the kiss of life. They will bash up and then kill someone else ... maybe the guy they meant to get, maybe me, maybe you. Maybe Eleanor. Tell me the truth, where does this assassin fellow fit in with your missing daughter? If you don't tell me the truth I can't help you.'

'We don't need help. My daughter's not missing and she doesn't know this dead man.'

But his voice was tightened in his throat.

I said, 'I know him. I don't know his name but I met him. The police blamed me for it at first, then they changed their minds. Today in the paper it says he shot Di Nemico...'

'It says nothing of the sort!'

'Stop being coy. Where are we, Charlie? I think we should meet.'

'You're making two plus two equals five.'

'Two plus two coppers equals five. The French police obviously think he shot Di Nemico or was mixed up in it. Eleanor is connected to him.'

'No. You're wrong. Now I've really got to go.'

'Okay. Don't you want to know why I read today's *Standard*?'

'Tell me.'

'I went for a drink when I got back. Met a newshound friend of mine. He said, "How are you, Jimmy? I thought you were in jail." "What makes you think that?" says I. "Oh, our Paris man said it to the fellow on the next desk to me. He said he'd had a whisper the French police were interviewing an English private detective. Anti-terrorist squad. Bloke with a walking-stick, that was the whisper he had, only the Paris correspondent couldn't print that because the French police would get cheesed off with him." The journalist I met presumed it was me, Charlie, since I answered the description. I told him to think again. I don't know if he's convinced; London's hardly chock-a-block with one-legged private detectives.'

'Did you tell him you were in Paris?'

'We weren't in Paris, we were in Islington.'

'Turn that bloody row down!' screamed one of my neighbours; his voice, like the ghetto-blaster, muted by my window glass. 'Don't you know what the time is?'

I looked out. The kids waved up to my neighbour but kept playing the blaster, only now they were laughing. I laughed too.

'It's not funny. Was he on a fishing trip or did he really have a lot of stuff about you and the Paris police?'

'Couldn't say. It's one of the things I was hoping to discuss with you. Still, if you're not about to see me...'

There was a silence.

'Come and have breakfast. My golf club does a good one. Meet me there at six tomorrow and we'll play a few holes first. It's the North Surrey Gentlemen's. Woking.'

'Six! You must be having me on. Nine is my best offer.'

'Six-thirty. Get there on time, though. I'll put you straight about all this. And don't go blabbing to any journalists. Promise me that for now.'

'I'll have the breakfast. Forget the golf. I can't play golf. No one plays on a false leg.'

'Rubbish. I knew a bloke played with one hand. Low handicapper, too. Only used irons, no woods. You turn up at six-thirty and mum's the word to journalists, okay? Have a few holes. Set you up for breakfast.'

'Who cooks at your golf club, a night shift?'

After I put the phone down I got to thinking... *one hand*? A few swings with the walking-stick did nothing to convince me. The sound of the ghetto-blaster faded into the night. A police car was parked by the streetlamp. The kids had gone. I drank some whisky and flipped around the TV channels, looking for an old film and failing to find one. I settled for an Open University Module on Soil Mechanics. I still don't know what it is.

Chapter Twenty-four

Leon had done a beautiful job on the Rover, which he said had needed valves grinding. It purred. He growled. He complained about being dragged out of bed to give it back to me. I complained that mere valve grinding should cost so much. Teeth grinding. He said I should see what a new crank for one of these buggers cost if I was worried about cost, and also a man couldn't find a class-A mechanic who came cheaper than Leon did. He stood in the dusty little yard behind his workshop and grinned, bleary-eyed, as he boasted of his prowess with a spanner. I couldn't even buy a sidelight bulb from Leon without hearing the speech.

'It's a nice day, Jim-boy.'

'It certainly is. It's going to be a hot one.'

He nodded. 'Where you going at such a rush?'

'Surrey.'

'Surrey!' He shook his head. He was small and very dark and very West Indian, though his features were an Asian's. 'You get around, mate. Paris, Surrey. You're a jet setter, Jim-boy. Next thing, you'll be affording a decent motor.'

Next thing I was in the Brixton traffic jam, trying to make my way over to Tooting and all points south. At eight-thirty I was on the Kingston bypass. The morning was hot but not as hot as Paris had been. The arid, continental air had gone and in its place was a faint westerly Atlantic breeze. A balmy-feeling English summer's day on the way. We all have our fantasies, and being in my olde English car in my olde English homeland is one of mine. The metalwork of my Rover was so hot it stung my hand to touch. The leather seats smelled like the insides of cars should, old and waxy and well tanned. I turned the radio down to a background burble. My hands rested on the steering-wheel and the sunshine rested on my hands. The only possible advantage of 'abroad' is sunshine, and today we had sunshine in England. Bliss.

A car horn blasted and a purple-faced man in a big black BMW passed, shaking his fist and yelling something. Something rude. The car behind me flashed his headlamps and tooted his horn too. Suddenly everyone's in a hurry to Surrey. The Kingston bypass doesn't ever have more than three fatal accidents per day, which makes you wonder what's so good about Surrey that everyone's killing themselves to get there. I got there soon enough for my taste.

*

The North Surrey Gentlemen's was a lush green number with a 1920s clubhouse faked up to look like a Palladian villa, a freshly tarmacadamed car-park, and regimented evergreens all around to protect both from mis-hit balls. As I drove in, a walnut-faced flunkey in blue working-clothes was sweeping imaginary litter into a pan and overseeing the wall-to-wall fancy cars. He gave me one of those 'what are *you* doing here' stares. Obviously they don't get many fifteen-year-old Rovers. I spotted the black Beemer that had passed me on the Kingston bypass. Old purple-face was probably half-way round the course by now, cursing the fellow in front for taking time over his putting.

'Can I help?' asked the wrinkled walnut.

'Probably not, cocker. I'm looking for a geezer called Wallace. I'm supposed to meet him here.'

I waved at the car-park. It was empty save for the old boy, me and a million quid's worth of motors. I couldn't see Charlie's hired Ford. The walnut smiled.

'He's out on the course, sir. He asked me to tell you he waited for you. He's signed you in and arranged some clubs for you. They're on the trolley outside the pro's shop. Blue bag. The green fee's paid.'

'Clubs?'

'Over there, sir.' He pointed through the evergreens to a modern building half-hidden in a copse.

'How long's he been gone?'

102

'A while. You'll find him, oh I'd say on the fourth or fifth. That's the way to the fourth green.' He pointed again, this time into bright, blinding sunlight. 'And just in case he's still on the third, you follow that line of trees from the fourth green. You'll see. Don't stand still for too long.' He laughed.

I walked into the sunlight, trusting the old man's directions.

'What about the clubs?' the old man called. 'The pro's shop's this way.'

'You have them.'

*

I didn't walk more than three miles before I found Charlie, nor was I shouted at more than a dozen times by BMW owners. Even when I stood still they never seemed to get the ball to go more than fifty yards. Charlie was watching one of these experts when I found him.

'Jimmy,' he whispered, 'good to see you. Didn't they tell you about the clubs?'

'I was told.' I tugged his sleeve and led him away from the tee. 'Are you with them?'

The man preparing to strike the ball was dressed all in salmon-pink; salmon-pink golfing slacks, socks, sports shirt and bandanna. Where else in England but a yacht marina or a golf course could a person wear a bandanna? He wore white shoes with frills on the front, and only needed mayonnaise and cucumber to garnish. His companion was slightly more restrained in a lime-green shirt, red golfer's cap and white slacks.

'No I'm not. I told them to play through. I was taking my time and waiting for you.' Charlie limped away from me so he could get a clear view of where the striker's shot went. Beside the men playing through, Charlie was positively sober in a navy-blue cotton ensemble, contrasting white piping and black shoes, no frills.

'Thanks for waiting. I did tell you I only wanted breakfast. No golf.'

'Quiet!' Charlie said, a stage whisper.

The salmon-pink player looked around at me, then, satisfied I would stay quiet, drew his club back and gave the ball an almighty 'thwack!' It landed in the middle of the fairway a couple of hundred yards on. I felt like applauding. The man in

the salmon-pink muttered and was unhappy with his shot, then
sheathed his club. The man in the lime-green shirt stood at the
tee, placed his ball and with no more ado repeated the trick. He
turned and looked at me.

'Nice one.' I put on a friendly face. '*Well* walloped.'

'I hope you're not sharing clubs, it's illegal here.'

'Just watching, he's just round for the walk,' Charlie said.

'Watch his etiquette, then, Mr?'

'Wallace. Watch yours, mister.'

The lime-green man turned nasty-looking, all frown and
wrinkled-up nose. 'What did you say?'

Charlie smiled. 'You're holding me up. There are people
following.'

'Very good. Positively waggish,' I said when the two
confections were out of earshot.

'Just stand well clear.'

I did. Charlie took a steel golf club out of his leather bag, lined
himself up on the ball, waggled the club head then took a heave.
He got that 'thwack!' sound too, only his ball went about a mile
in the air and landed in a little wood less than fifty yards from the
tee. Maybe I should have taken the clubs from the pro's shop.

'That's a Ballesteros, double wound. We'd better have a look
for it.'

'No kidding, Ballesteros double wound, eh?... we'd better.'
Even *I* know who Sevvy Ballesteros is. We limped towards the
little wood.

'I don't believe you ever lost her,' I said when we were in the
wood. Charlie didn't answer. He was thwacking with the golf
club again, only this time the beneficiaries of the thwacks were
tall clumps of grass that grew between the trees. Dew droplets
flew in sunlight that slanted through the green, narrow boughs
of the trees. Out on the brightly lit fairway some more men
dressed in highly coloured clothes were yelling at each other and
laughing and hitting balls not very far.

'Are we safe in here?' I asked.

'Should be.'

'That's what the other fellow said.'

'What other fellow?'

'All of them. The one your ball hit. It's probably the last thing
your daughter's boyfriend said before those guys chucked him
off his balcony... "Well, I should be safe enough around here."'

'Up yours, Jenner. I broke my tee peg back there and now I've lost my Sevvy.'

Charlie whacked a bush good and proper, then a clump of grass, then another bush. He was really angry. I'll never stop being surprised at how small sums of money can make people angry. I held up a brown envelope.

'I'm returning the price of as many golf balls as a man could ever want. Plus my account of my expenses. Plus one unused air ticket, tourist class, Paris to London. We'd better get things straight now, because your daughter's at the centre of a complicated situation. I think you haven't lost touch with your daughter. She was just doing something you didn't fancy and you decided to flush her out. You decided sticking Jenner's private detective nose into her life was a good way to impress her you were serious. I'd go round to the boyfriend's house, look tough and moody, boyfriend wets his underpants and sends daughter running home to Daddy. How's it sound?'

Charlie thwacked another bush.

'Only instead of that happening something goes terribly wrong... had in fact gone terribly wrong before I even arrived there only maybe you didn't know it. We both know the house I was sent to had a man in it who later turned up dead and we both know, whether you'll admit it nor not, we both know the report in the *Standard* and the way the French police treated me means they think that man was one of the ones who murdered this politician, Di Nemico. I can tie them together, I think, but I have to talk to Eleanor to get this straight.'

'Well you're wrong. You leave my daughter alone.'

He held the club tightly in his fists.

'Okay. I'll leave your daughter alone. I won't even try to talk to her. Whoever it was killed this boy in Paris, though, he won't. He didn't mash up his *own* feet with a hammer, he didn't chuck *himself* over the top of his landing...'

'Shut up!' He stood quivering for a few moments. I thought he would burst a blood vessel and keel over. Charles Wallace stared at me, on and on, then controlled himself. His face calmed, seemed to unstiffen. 'You finished? I want to find my ball.'

The brightly clothed men on the fairway were staring at us.

'Play through!' Charlie called. 'We've lost our ball.'

The men turned away.

105

'I told you the truth, Jenner. Okay, so she'd dropped out, I knew about it, I knew she was living in squats and hanging round with all sorts of shits. What was I supposed to do, eh? These people find out Eleanor's background, that she has an income, and they think, "She can bankroll us." That's what they think. Her godmother did me the kindness of keeping me informed. Juliette was on the spot in Paris, so she was in a position to know and she was in relatively regular contact with Eleanor. She kept in touch with me because you can't keep in touch with my ex-wife, who lives somewhere triangulated between the Beagle Channel, here and Cloud-cuckoo-land. She also doesn't have a phone and doesn't give a damn, okay?'

'Go on.'

'Go on what? *This* is why I'm living semi-permanently in London. To be available, which I can't do from the other side of the Atlantic. *This* is why I'm losing money hand over fist, when my career is going nicely again in America and I'm sitting in London turning parts down.'

Charlie brushed the bark of a fallen tree with his hand then sat. It was a big tree from before the younger ones were planted. We were in a managed tree-farm. The big tree came from an earlier life. It looked like a sculpture. I sat too.

'Eventually Eleanor came to me. I knew she would.'

'Why?'

He shrugged. 'I'm her father. I knew.'

'No. Why did she come? Who was she scared of?'

'I don't know.'

We sat in silence for a long time. White butterflies floated around us. The grass in the little wood smelled sweet. Outside I could hear more golfers. Eventually Charlie said, 'I wanted her to come home permanently.' His voice became fierce. '*I* should be the one she comes to, not some soapy joes rigged out in yellow frocks.'

'Yellow frocks?'

'She's got some chums in Paris.' Charlie Wallace stood. 'They wear yellow frocks, keep pictures of some dirty-looking Indian bugger round their necks, smoke pot and screw each other non-stop. Also they don't eat meat, I think. It's a terrible thing a girl's father has to come to terms with, Jimmy. Do you have any daughters?'

'I don't even have a wife anymore. No, no children. No daughters.'

106

'Good. Keep it that way, that's my advice. Only have sons. You'd need to be a dumb bastard to take advice from someone like me.' Charlie picked unhappily at dried and dead moss on the fallen tree which had been our seat, then turned away abruptly. 'Come on, Sevvy's flown to the great big fairway in the sky. I'd better get out here and drop a ball or I'll never finish this bloody round.'

We walked through the dappled shade to pick up Charlie's leather golf bag, then stepped out into brilliant sunlight again. The fairway was empty, a smooth green baize laid across the neatly forested countryside. In the distance the flag hung limp over the hole.

'This is tricky,' Charlie said. 'There's water down there but you can't see it because it lies in a shallow ditch. Once you're in there...' He shook his head, reached into his bag for a Sevvy and dropped it at arm's length. Charlie drew a steel club from his bag, lined himself up, waggled the club head then heaved at the Sevvy. The ball went straight for the shallow ditch, like a homing pigeon. Like a homing duck. As if it had been born to live in the waters of the dip with all the other amphibious golf balls.

'The French police had a theory that the fellows who murdered your daughter's boyfriend wore yellow. English speakers who wore yellow Indian clothes were spotted near where he was killed. Are you saying your daughter's pals murdered her murdering boyfriend? Is that it?'

'For the last time *he wasn't her boyfriend*!'

'Oh come on! Who was he then?'

Charlie slammed the club back into the leather bag, then rounded on me.

'He is a man who was staying in a flat. A squatter's flat, a drug culture flat, okay? The flat belonged to a French girl Lenny knew ages ago. The girl's disappeared, which is something you will probably have noticed drop-outs do. She is probably living in a commune and they've all probably got purple hair and dirty hands. I'm guessing, but that's how they all seem to end up. Eleanor and her boyfriend moved into the flat for a couple of weeks. Then they moved out again. Juliette gave you that address and she made a mistake in doing so. There's the muddle.'

'Why doesn't your daughter live in her own flat in rue Vaugirard?'

'*Exactly*. Let me know when you have an answer. Because people of her age are bloody perverse, is what I think. Because a clean modern apartment with all mod cons wouldn't fit her romantic view of herself.'

'She didn't look like a drop-out when I saw her. She just looked ordinary.'

'Well, there you go.'

Charlie began to limp towards the shallow ditch. I limped after him, speaking to his back.

'So it's just a coincidence that the next man into the flat in Saint-Denis was murdered?'

'Yes.'

'And the French police agree with you it was just a co-incidence?'

'Yes.' Called over his shoulder.

'And they believe he was the man who shot Di Nemico?'

'That's what you say. I don't know.'

He stopped and turned to face me. I said, 'And it was a coincidence he was murdered on the same day as I visited him? And it was a coincidence I was given the wrong address on just that day? And it was a coincidence that the French police thought at first that he'd been killed by men in yellow frocks? And it was a coincidence that everywhere I went in Paris I was getting checked out by French policemen, all the time . . . that was just a coincidence?'

He nodded.

'Well, Charlie, some things are wrong here. I didn't get the address from Juliette, as you seem to think. I got it from a young American who knows Eleanor. A fellow called Tom Smith. *She* gave *him* the address. Check your facts, Charlie, especially if you're going to lie to me. The next thing that is wrong is the French coppers. They must be pretty starstruck with you to believe all this tosh . . . that is *if* they do believe it. I personally think they do not and never did. Also they didn't just change their minds about me; they threw me out of France before there was a chance for me to become an embarrassment by asking a load of questions or perhaps even providing an investigating magistrate with some answers they might prefer he didn't hear. Next is the fact that you are scared that I might blabbo to a journalist; I mean, I thought you were going to burst into tears last night on the blower. Last, but not least, is the fact that the French secret service or something like it had me babysat all the

108

way back to London... *all* the way. Why should they do that? I ask myself. The answer is of course that I am carrying some answers here, and they want to know what I will do with them. I am going home now to figure out what it is I'm supposed to know. My advice is that you should do the same thing, and think up a better story. So far you're insulting my intelligence.'

'Secret service?'

I mopped my brow with my handkerchief.

'Yes. Maybe one of these trees is spying on us or maybe hidden in the boot of my car. Young, nice-looking girl with short dark hair. Sounds like a Yank but she's French Canadian or the like. Stuck to me like flypaper all the way to London. When you decide to play straight give me a call. Meanwhile...' I felt very tired suddenly. 'Meanwhile I haven't had any breakfast. Meanwhile dig your Sevvy out of the haha. Meanwhile... where's your car?'

'I had a problem with some roadworks in Maida Vale.'

I strode away. Before I'd gone far I was among the fores and flying golf balls. It took me a while to find the car-park again and a while longer to start my car. I had to have the bonnet up and poke around its innards before it would even make a coughing noise. I don't really know what the hell's under the bonnet. I mean, I know this one's the carburettor and this one's the distributor cap, the sump's down there and here's a load of wires and metal gubbins in-between. The gubbins stank of petrol, the wires looked as if they were on annual leave and all the metalwork looked hard and unforgiving... *resentful*. Why have you neglected me so badly, Jenner? Why not give me a service every six months? Don't I deserve better than a rusting exhaust which would work better as a colander? Where's Leon? I like Leon. He's *nice* to me.

This is neither the time nor the place to discuss it, car. I stood by its side smoking a cigarette I found in the glove-box and staring at the underside of the bonnet, so as not to catch old walnut-face's eye. Actually I don't smoke. After ten minutes the car started anyway, so getting some air did it the world of good. It's just getting old now, that car, and it don't like the heat anymore.

Me neither.

*

Outside the North Surrey Gentlemen's Golf Club is a lay-by. It's marked up as a picnic area, and if you were the kind of picnicker who liked dusty sandwiches and hydrocarbon soup it would suit you just fine. A blue car was parked alone in the lay-by. It looked like a rental car. Its driver was a young woman; short dark hair, slim petite woman. Almost like a teenager. I only glimpsed her. As I drove past she found something of urgent interest under the dash. What's interesting under the dash of a rented Ford Escort? I couldn't imagine. I drove slowly back to London, and I spent a lot of time looking in the rear-view mirror, but I didn't see her again. Paranoia, Jenner, I told myself. Why would Eleanor be here?

Chapter Twenty-five

The car expired on the Chertsey Road. I spent too long looking in that rear-view mirror for girls who weren't there, and the next I knew Mr Rover's gauge is on the red and steam is coming from under his bonnet. I walked a mile looking for a phone-box that worked, then sat in the car for another ninety minutes waiting for Leon and a tow-truck that never came. I read a Christmas '74 edition of the *Daily Mirror* I found under the boot mat. It's no way for a grown man to spend his day. I left the keys in the car and walked into Richmond, taking a more contemporary newspaper into a boozer on Richmond Green. Outside were the yuppies, soaking up the sun, 'Yah yah yah, BMW, 'nother Martini, dear?' Inside was Jenner, smouldering into a first-class temper over a few pints of beer. I hate Richmond. By early evening I was in Frith Street, Soho, with a bunch of fellows who make a career of reeling round the pubs and clubs there. I've never figured out what they all do for money, but those fellows drink okay. So did I. I saw four more girls who looked like Eleanor or maybe like French Canadian Mandy, all in different places and all dressed differently. A couple more drinks and I'd have been mistaking young men and little old ladies for her. My intention was to forget Charlie and Eleanor Wallace, forget about French cops and the bodies of dead young men. By dusk I'd nearly managed it, and was walking across Trafalgar Square looking for a lavatory. I wondered if I wasn't hallucinating when Eleanor stood suddenly full in front of me.

'Not everything is right there out in the open, Jimmy Jenner. Not everything can be seen straight off.'

111

'You can say that again, sport.'

'The situation you are in is only seen by you in a fragmentary way . . .'

'Maybe.'

'Not maybe . . . *always.*'

'You're young enough to philosophise. In common with older men everywhere I am obsessed by practicalities.'

'What?'

'I'm looking for a lavatory.'

'Other people have views. It's important you respect them. It's important you don't just blunder into people's lives.'

She worked her fingers as she spoke, but she looked calm enough.

'I based my career on just these premises. I seem to remember it was *you* who asked me to look after your father, and it was *your father* who asked me to find you. I didn't volunteer for either job.'

'But not anymore. You don't need to bother anymore. We're in contact, thank you.'

'Do you have a blue Ford Escort?'

Eleanor shook her head.

'Didn't there used to be some lavvies down here?'

'Some people want absolutely everything explained to them. As if they have a right to it. Some people aren't willing to accept what you do at face value. My father's one. Some people won't accept that if you need to go away, sooner or later you *will* go away. It's as simple as that.'

'What attitude did your chum in Paris strike over the matter? I reckon your going away must have left him so distraught he mashed up his own feet and then slung himself out of your flat.'

'It's not my flat.'

'You know the bloke I mean, then?'

She didn't speak for a while, then she said, 'Charlie would not accept that I had to go and make a life of my own. I don't know why because he had hardly smothered me with his company before.'

'Perhaps it wasn't *what* you were doing but the *way* you did it and the *who* you did it with.'

'People need to be trusted. I need to be trusted to run my own life.'

'That's what I should have said to Letellier. Do you know him?'

'No.'

St Martin's churchyard . . . of course. There's one of those big ribbed-concrete lavatories with a pneumatic door – imported from France, too. The ten-pence pee – it's not just in Stoke Newington you get muggers. I marched up to the churchyard, tailed by the revenant Eleanor. I was surprised she was still there when I came out again. Few of my hallucinations last so long. Eleanor was sitting calmly on a little green bench. I came through the pneumatic door reeling from the combined effect of the alcohol, the smell of Harpic and the fact that I'd just peed into a glass-fibre loo accompanied by James Last and his Orchestra.

'Can I come home with you?' she said.

'Where have you been?'

'I spent last night at George's flat, in Wapping. You remember George Tiler?'

'How could I forget him? Has he written you any letters . . . don't tell me. But if he has, send them back unopened. That's my advice, otherwise you'll be followed around by characters like me offering you money to leave the country. Do you have an answering machine?'

'No.'

'Just as well. Never answer his messages.'

'His messages were about me, Jimmy. I wanted to see you. I wanted to speak.'

'Why have you waited so long to talk to me?'

She laughed. 'You weren't easy to find. Then you weren't easy to approach. Take me to your flat and we'll talk as much as you want.'

'Why was I difficult to approach?'

'You were being followed. You're not now.'

'Why have they gone?'

She shrugged but did not speak.

'Have you got a couple of pounds, Eleanor?'

'Why?'

'I've drunk all my money. Westminster City Council's just had the last ten pee. I can't even remember my money-card number. I was going to walk home. If you can pay the tube fares to Manor House, you can come home with me.'

'Deal.'

We plunged into the neon-lit nightmare under Coutts bank. Two dirty-looking young men, obviously there for the night and several past, drank Carlsberg Special in a subterranean shop doorway, leaning giggling against each other and calling after us for money.

'Got the price of a cup of tea, mate?'

A young European woman wearing Indian-style clothes stood by a line of smashed public telephones. She was waiting for someone, I thought. Us? While she waited she read from a small and well-thumbed paperback book. A photograph of either a yeti or a very hairy guru hung on a chain of wooden beads and nestled between her large, cotton-covered, unslung breasts. I believe that's most gurus' aim in life. Yetis I don't know about.

'One of your lot?' I said, nodding at the girl.

'Here's your ticket. Did you know those men?'

'Ouch!'

*

On the tube station platform yellow demon lights flickered above us. The train wheels smashed the calm of the subterranean station. Eleanor said something I didn't catch. The doors 'shushed' closed behind us, and she repeated it.

'You shouldn't get drunk like that. It's bad for you.'

Beware of innocent-looking girls with sharp tongues, Jenner.

'Living is bad for you, Eleanor.'

Beware of easy money, I thought. Nothing is for nothing. I leaned my head against the glass of the tube-train window. As the train started a woman dashed on to the platform, just too late. She was dark-haired, sharply dressed. She was slim and petite. I wondered where she'd left her Ford. Then we were in the tunnel and we'd left her alone on the platform. I stared into the train-carriage window.

'What is it?' Eleanor asked, frowning.

'Beware of the French. Beware of foreigners generally. A girl is only safe in England. Even then, beware of men in yellow frocks.'

'Beware of booze,' she countered. A man in a business suit opposite stared at us. I held Eleanor's hand and the man looked away.

'Beware of the Big Foot, Eleanor, and beware of gurus everywhere.'

'Beware of booze,' she repeated. 'You need some coffee, Jenner.'

114

Chapter Twenty-six

She wore a light, sea-island cotton pale pink dress and a cream-coloured, starchy, thick-linen jacket. The jacket was faded but I believe it was meant to be; a fashion. She sat on my battered leather sofa where she'd sat just a few weeks before and she smiled a soft smile and looked like that same mixture of innocence and seduction, only older. I don't mean 'older' in the sense that time makes us older. She looked knowing, somehow. Maybe it had been there all the time, but I hadn't seen it the first time round.

Eleanor Wallace had dyed her hair deep brown, almost black, and she'd had it cut short so it flattened against her skull like a boy's, or looked like a nun's might without her habit. Looked like I always imagined Joan of Arc's hair. Eleanor was too thin. She sat with her knees close together and her big eyes watched me while I made coffee. The night was hot and the barometer was rising. A great column of pressure lay over the city, a mountain of still air resting on us. So much for gentle English breezes. Outside my flat the kids' ghetto-blasters pounded as if we were in Kingston, Jamaica waiting for Hurricane Jimmy. A group of youngsters, the same ones as the night before plus others, had collected in the streetlamp's pool of light. The sweet smell of dope drifted up to my window.

'Charlie's not a very good liar,' Eleanor said. 'It's a strange thing, given his work, but it's the truth. He can't fake to people.'

The Moka machine spilled coffee over my hand. It misbehaves as if it has a will of its own. As if my ex-wife who gave it to me for my birthday had had it invested with devils first. I'd drunk too much booze, of course. I held my hand under the cold tap and left the coffee machine to boil dry. Eleanor laughed and stood to turn it off.

'Forget the coffee. It doesn't matter.'

I poured two whiskies and we sat.

'No ice. I never have any made. I don't know why.'

'I don't drink. Tell me about your adventures.'

She smiled, as if she was some friendly job interviewer.

'My adventures, Miss Eleanor, are quiet compared with yours. I am not being sought by Interpol.'

'Nor am I or my father wouldn't have hired you.'

'And I'm not tied in with any dead men.'

'Oh no? That wasn't the impression I got in your hotel. The police there looked as if you were quite important to them. They looked as if they were arresting a possibly violent suspect.'

'So how come they didn't arrest you too?'

'They weren't looking for me. I was just a girl sitting in an hotel foyer when they picked you up. That's not a crime.'

'Okay. Then your father tells me you've moved in with a lover in France.'

'Down to earth at last. You sound like somebody's grandmother . . . is it because you're jealous or something?'

'Let your father be jealous of you. And let him be approving or otherwise. I won't. I just wanted to get a grip of where you stand in this mess. As far as I'm concerned you have my full permission to go and wreck your own life . . . if you ever wanted my permission.'

'I'm wrecking nothing.'

'Of course. That's how I see it.'

'Don't be sarcastic.'

'I'm not. Either you want to talk to me or you don't. Either you're going to explain what you've been up to or not. I can't force you to and I don't think your father ever had it in mind that I should.'

'Of course he did. You were his apeman, all set to drag me back by the hair. What else do you think he hired you for?'

I looked at the pink cotton dress and wondered. Charlie's comments on the golf course made sense . . . don't have daughters if you can help it.

'Tell me about the man in the flat. What was his name?'

'Paolo. Paolo Bianchi.'

'Someone is pulling Jenner's leg,' I said. 'I *know* Paolo

Bianchi, at least I've met him, and he doesn't look like that fellow did.'

'Someone is not. You've met the one Leila's got her tentacles around, I guess?'

'Yes. I met him with her at George Tiler's.'

She frowned. 'What does George Tiler have to do with it?'

'Nothing as far as I know. I just met Bianchi at George's country house with about a million horsey types, Leila and a couple of his London friends. My car failed and Bianchi's driver brought me home. Who is the other one?'

'His son. *Was* his son.'

'And you knew him?'

'Yes.'

'Ooh ooh, Eleanor. How well?'

'Very well. We were old friends and I went to stay with him in Italy this spring. This entire business started with Paolo. Paolo the younger, I mean. He drove me from Bologna to Paris. At least that was the plan. We took the wriggly route through the Alps. Somewhere in France, a long way off the beaten track, we were stopped by some border police and two detectives. The border police drove away pretty soon and left us with the two detectives, who had turned us out of the car. They were absolutely vile to us and arrested us.'

I held up my hand for her to stop.

'Red, red wine', roots-rockers-style, came floating up from the street with the sweet-smelling weed. I stood and looked out of the window. The kids were in clinches and drifting in and out of the pool of light, could only be separated by judicious use of a bucket of cold water and a crowbar. One boy, a runt, the odd one out, danced alone to the music, eyes closed and woolly hat pulled low on his forehead. His arms swung slowly by his sides. He looked comfortable. The boy was about eleven or twelve. The other kids might have been two years older. Eleanor was maybe five years older than them. The children smooching in the street and the child-woman sitting on my sofa made me feel ... out of touch, I guess. There goes old man Jenner. Mind what you say in front of him. He's *old*. I turned away from the window and let the blind snap.

'Not so fast. *How* did you meet the Bianchi kid?'

'I knew him a long time ago. Absolutely years.'

I looked into her beautiful young face and wondered how long 'absolutely years' meant.

'So you're in this lonely valley. Aosta or somewhere.'

'Miles further. Right in France. The French detectives beat us up a bit, then ripped Paolo's car apart. Like animals. They claimed to have found a load of stuff in the car.'

'Stuff?'

'Cocaine.'

'You said "claimed". Was it?'

'They arrested us so I expect it was. They threw us in the back of the van. Started hitting Paolo and trying to get information from him. They were very mean, Jimmy Jenner.'

'I suppose they were a bit fed up. Where was this stuff they found?'

'In the seat backs.'

'Did you see it?'

She nodded.

'They took us out of the van and showed it to us.'

'Whose was it?'

'Not mine. Not his he claimed. He was very vociferous, very angry about it. He said he was being framed. Paolo was very, very clear that he was being framed. The policemen simply threw us back in the van and started driving. We drove for – I don't know. Hours and hours. We were driven back towards Paris. Then they stopped the van and took me out. I was terrified.'

'I'm sure.'

'I didn't know what they would do. You know, the French police have a reputation.'

'Don't they? So let's get this clear. The van stopped in Paris and they took you out, yes?'

'No. They stopped *near* Paris. In a wood. It was about dawn and we'd been driven all night with no seats and no blankets. We'd just rattled around in the back of the van. I was so sore and confused, Jimmy. And these two French policemen took me out of the van, gave me a cigarette and said, "Relax, we can do a deal."'

'Letellier and Meyer, is that who they were?'

'No, those weren't the names.'

'What did they look like?'

'Young. Dark. Very well dressed. They could have been brothers or something. Both aged under thirty, I think. One wore Givenchy aftershave. Tons of it.'

118

I went to speak but she held her finger up.

'The next part is the most important. You see, they didn't seem to be interested in Paolo. They were interested in *me*. They were interested in people I knew. People quite apart from Paolo, you know.'

'The guys in the yellow dresses?'

Eleanor shook her head.

'When I was younger I was part of a circle of friends, well they weren't necessarily *my* friends. I didn't know them all. But I had a boyfriend at the time.'

'*Another* boyfriend?'

'Another.'

'And let me get this straight, please. You're saying you were part of a circle of friends not all of whom you *knew*? How can that be?'

'I mean I knew this fellow and he was one of quite a few young people in Paris in those days who were into radical politics.'

'Radical politics? You mean radical *non*-politics, I take it?'

'I don't know.'

She worked her fingers. I finished my whisky and started on hers. The music stopped outside.

'Well, when people say "radical politics" in England they mean belonging to the Co-operative Party. You don't mean that, do you?'

'I didn't know then exactly what they were like. I knew Tom and his friends were a little bit crazy. Can I have a cigarette?'

'I don't smoke. I don't keep them.'

'You sound as if you don't approve, Jenner.'

'Of course I don't. *How* crazy were these friends you didn't know?'

She stood and walked around the room, stretching her arms and yawning.

'Pigs' heads, that sort of thing. That's how crazy.'

'What pigs' heads?'

'They used to nail pigs' heads to synagogue doors. Or paint "PLO" on walls.'

'Are we talking about the Tom I met? The scruffy bloke who met me when you didn't turn up? Newspaper fellow?'

She nodded.

'I hadn't seen them for absolutely ages. Six months at least, and it was even longer than that that I broke up with Tom.'

'How much longer?'

'A while. But I was only a kid really when I was with Tom. I was still at school . . . can you believe that? He was twenty-seven.'

'How long ago was that?'

'I left a year ago in July.'

'Some school. Where was it?'

'Neuilly-sur-Seine.' Eleanor smiled briefly. 'It was a convent school.'

'And the nuns let you fall in love with a radical politics American boy in Paris when they were supposed to be getting you into university?'

'No. The nuns didn't "let" me fall in love with Tom – who is not, by the way, American but French and spent a period of his childhood in California where his mother taught French. That's how come he uses an American name. It's a game with him. Anyhow, there was never any question of the nuns educating me for a university. The nuns were educationalists of the intact hymen school of thought, and deportment and all that shit. Does it shock you when I say "shit"?'

'Please. I'll let you know clear enough when I'm shocked. So far I'm not shocked. Any surprises – not "shocks" – you have given me depend more on what you do than what you say. Okay? Say "shit" if it suits you. I personally think it doesn't.'

'Shit, Jimmy, that's a silly comment.' She stared at me. I didn't react. 'And saying the nuns "let" me fall in love – if falling in love was what it was – also stinks, while we're clearing up your attitudes.'

'What was the deal?'

'Oh . . . that we didn't have to go to prison. They said there was enough stuff in the car to put Paolo away for twenty years and me for something similar. He would get slightly longer because he owned the car. And they said Paolo didn't have to serve twenty years or even five minutes and neither did I as long as we co-operated. Me in particular. As long as *I* co-operated, because it was me really they were doing the deal with. These two policemen said what they wanted to do was catch a dangerous gang who had done political assassinations and the like for two years past, and they'd already had a member of the gang, a girl called Claudine. I remembered Claudine, too, when they described her. They said that I would be taken to meet the policemen in charge of the operation against this dangerous gang of political assassins but first I would have to agree to take part in the operation, or face the consequences of Paolo and myself being found with the drugs, you see? Tom and his friends were the "gang" these detectives were after and Claudine was their informant. I laughed in their faces when they told me. What a joke! But the two policemen didn't laugh. They said they had information that Tom and Claudine and a boy called Jean-Marie Chantin that I didn't know then and a German that I did, a man called Verner, Bruno Verner, were responsible for the murder of a trade union official in Lyons.'

'Trade union officials and synagogues . . . these people are surprisingly even-handed, don't you think? You're too far ahead for me anyway. Let's stick with this remote valley. How come two French detectives happen to stop you in a remote valley and put all this "we-want-to-have-you-do-this-and-that" stuff to you? It seems unlikely. I mean it wasn't by chance, Eleanor. And how come they knew they'd have the drop on you? How come they *knew* they'd find illegal substances?'

'About the cocaine; I don't know. But I never had anything to do with it so I don't know anything which could help explain that. About where we were; well, I expect that came straight-forwardly from Tom Smith via Claudine. I'd told someone who knew Tom well that I was going to come with Paolo Bianchi from Italy back to Paris and I'd said when I was going to arrive in Paris. Presumably that person told Tom and Tom told Claudine. That's what I believe must have been the route for the information to the coppers.'

'And what was the route for the information that the car you were in was full of naughty substances? How did they know that?'

'I can't say. I just don't know. The main point is that they wanted someone close to Tom and his friends, and Claudine gave my name as someone who might be right for them, the bitch. We'd been trailed all the way, I'm sure. That cow.'

'Go right ahead.'

'That shit.'

'Fine, fine. What about her, why didn't they use her?'

'I don't know. Too stupid, I suppose, or perhaps they were frightened she'd tell Tom and the boys just like she'd told them. Maybe she wanted a fresh start. I don't know. She didn't get it.'

'What happened next? We're in a wood near Paris and these

two young policemen have just offered you a deal to get you and your boyfriend off a charge of cocaine smuggling. What was your response?'

'I wanted a better deal. I wanted to know exactly what was expected of me before I agreed to anything. I wanted them to agree that Paolo must under no circumstances be kept in prison while I helped them. I said that I wanted a signed agreement that there would be no proceedings taken against us once these detectives had what they wanted. Obviously, it was the easiest thing in the world for them to say, yes you can do this, yes you can do that, and then renege on it once they'd got what they wanted.'

'Let's stop here a minute, Eleanor, because some of what you're saying doesn't make sense.'

'I need a cigarette.'

'I told you, there are none.'

'Well I need one.' She stood and paced the room. She was uncomfortable and edgy, but it wasn't just from the lack of a cigarette.

'The only conclusion that could be reached from what you're saying is that Paolo Bianchi, despite anything he said to the contrary, *knew* he was carrying cocaine. *Knew* it. He knew it and they knew he knew it. It's the only way the two detectives would have been absolutely A1, one-hundred-per-cent certain of getting a deal out of you once they'd picked you up. Do you follow me? Stopping you on spec would simply have given the game away. These fellows didn't stop you on spec. They stopped you all prepared to offer you a deal, and the only way they could have been that prepared is if they had good information that you and Paolo had a car full of a substance other than petroleum spirit *and that Paolo knew it*. Could this Claudine have been the source for that information?'

'I don't see how. I can accept she might have known that I was travelling from Italy to France because I'd told someone she knew. She might well have known I was with Paolo from the same source. But she couldn't have known that stuff was in our car from that source because *I* didn't know it and consequently I hadn't told the person.'

'Who was the person?'

'I don't want to say. I don't want to mix her up in this.'

'Juliette?'

'I don't want to say, okay?'

'Well, from wherever, they'd have had to have had the information. But you'd better sit down, because there's something else.'

'I don't want to sit.'

She threw the window open and leaned out, taking her weight on her forearms.

'Okay. Don't. But there's another conclusion I'm forced to, and I don't think you're going to like it. You see, if the policemen knew Paolo and you were carrying cocaine and they offered you a deal and you took it, it's impossible to believe anything other than that you knew too. *You* personally. *You* personally knew Paolo and you were carting this stuff into France. No mistake. No accident, no "*Surprise, surpri-ise! Well who the hell put that lot in there?*" Because if it had been the case that you really hadn't known, if *that* was the truth, you'd have told them to get lost. You would not have done any ballroom dancing with young French detectives in Parisian forests. You'd have said, "Up yours, mate. See you in court." You'd have said that. Anyone would. Anyone would at the *very least* insist on seeing a lawyer. I don't believe a person who really had nothing to fear would have agreed to such a half-arsed plan in some forest glade just because it was put to them. You must have believed they had something to hang on you *and* a way of hanging it on you. A way that both you and they would know would stick, because obviously as a young woman of previously good character with a private income and a very well-known father, your side of it would look pretty good in court. You *are* of previously good character?'

A smile. 'Yes.'

'And your friend?'

'Paolo's got . . . Paolo *had* a record for drugs.'

'An extensive one or was he once caught in the same room as a man smoking a joint? I mean there's a long way between a dope bust and being caught with a car full of coke.'

'Medium extensive.'

'In France?'

'In Italy.'

'But he was obviously known to the French police?'

'It looks like it, Jimmy.'

'So, Eleanor, we come to the crux of this. We come to what has led you to develop some strange behaviour and me to flinch every time I walk past a policeman. You have been keeping much rougher company than the nuns would have liked you to, and we are not talking hymens, swearwords, bunking off your Latin prep or treating your father like a distant relative. We are talking about coke busts and dead Italian coke dealers in Saint-Denis, I believe. Am I right?'

'If you want to look at it like that, yes.'

'And that's the way the French coppers saw it, I'm sure. What was their response when you made the demands?'

'They compromised over Paolo. They said he didn't have to wait in custody, that he could wait instead at some place where they could keep an eye on him. Paolo suggested the flat of an old girlfriend of mine, which was unoccupied owing to her having gone abroad for a while. To Goa. Paolo suggested her flat in Saint-Denis when the plan was put to him. He was very relieved. He thought they were going to put him in prison for a thousand years. He was very emotional.'

The phone rang. Leon.

'I want you to come over here right now,' he said.

'I'm busy at the moment. Did you get my car?'

'I did indeed, Jim-boy. Which is why you've got to come over here.'

'I can't. Could you deliver it?'

'No. When can you get here?' Leon sounded less than completely cool for once.

'Not till the morning.'

'This is pretty urgent, Jim-boy. I want you to come over here now.'

'However urgent it seems, it's not as urgent as what I'm doing, Leon. I can assure you.'

'It is. It really is. It's so urgent I can't tell you about it on the phone.'

'Nine a.m. Did you manage to fix it?'

'Yes. The bottom hose was split. I don't know where it got that from because it certainly never had it the last time *I* had hold of your car, Jim-boy, which is less than twenty-four hours ago.'

'Good. I'm glad you've fixed it. We'll talk in the morning. I'll come over and we'll discuss it at length. I'm sorry, Leon, but I've really got to go now.'

'You should come here, Jim-boy. It's a matter of life and death.'

'So's this. Bye now.'

I put the handset down.

'I'm tired,' Eleanor said.

'So am I. You met the man who was organising whatever it was these two policemen wanted you to do, right?'

'I did. That same morning. In an office block at the back of rue La Fayette.'

'Where exactly?'

'Rue Bleue. 171 rue Bleue. Near the Square Montholon. 171 is a relatively modern building, early fifties, I think, and these two policemen took me in a side entrance and up to the top floor. There was a small office with a middle-aged man in it.'

'Describe him.'

'I want some cigarettes.'

'Describe the man first.'

'You sound like him. Don't you trust me? Do you think I'll run away and never come back?'

'It's not that. I want to know.'

'*I* want some cigarettes.'

'So get some. There are keys on the mantelshelf. Go and get some.'

'Aren't you worried I won't come back?'

'Of course not. I'm not your keeper, Eleanor.'

She took the keys and pulled on her linen jacket.

'I won't be long.'

'I know you won't.'

'Really I won't.'

I opened the blind and pointed into the street. 'There's a garage down there, if you cross the pelican crossing and turn right. When you get down to the High Street you turn left and head for Stamford Hill. The garage is about two-fifty yards on your left-hand side. They sell them.'

'Aren't you worried about letting me go?'

'I'm worried you'll get mugged.'

'I won't get mugged.'

'Okay, you won't. I'll see you in ten minutes.'

The door clicked and then I saw her cross the road on the pelican crossing. After ten minutes she didn't come back and then after half an hour she didn't. After an hour I went to bed, contenting myself with the knowledge that I was not her keeper and not her jailer, just like I'd said. If her own father couldn't get

Eleanor to turn up when she said she was going to I don't believe my writ was going to run far with her. She was turning out, as my old Granny used to say, 'she's turning out to be a bit of a wild one'. Of course my Granny meant women who left their husbands, not fathers.

*

The rain came during the night. It had to come soon. There's an oceanful of the stuff floating just off the left-hand side of us, so it never stays sunny for long in England. If it's not raining it's just about to. I woke during the night feeling cramped and hungry and carrying a big headache. I had one thin sheet over me and I was sweating. The rain plop-plop-plopped on the outer window-sill and on the glass. Then a steady splashing came from the street outside. A car passed. Its wheels made a sloshing sound as it travelled through the rainwater. Its lights swept the ceiling over my head. Slosh-slosh-slosh, brakes squeal slowly at the junction, lights change to red, peep-peep-peep goes the alarm for the pedestrian crossing. All night, every night, peep-peep-peep. The next flat I live in is going to be nowhere near a road junction. It will have no famous antecedents. It will be faceless and nameless, somewhere in an anonymous metropolitan borough. No one will rip off your car outside. The neighbours will be polite, good-mannered and deferential to me. There will be no pelican crossing. Peep-peep-peep! Someone crosses the road outside. I lay there half-asleep and half-awake, too lazy to get up and make some food or even pop an aspirin.

*

Some time after the rain started Eleanor sat on my bed. I heard the door catch click and then her feet padding across the floor.

'How do you feel?'

Her voice whispered in the darkness behind me. I turned.

'Better. Much better. Somewhere between mild jaundice and medium severe bruising of the liver. I'm not used to that drinking business anymore. You reach an age and you can't take it.'

'What age?'

'Mine.'

She was silent. I said, 'Where have you been?'

She didn't answer.

I reached out to her. Eleanor was naked and shivered.

'Can I come in?' she said. She slipped under the duvet.

'Where are your clothes?'

'Soaking wet. Do you mind?'

'No. I don't mind.'

'I feel scared, Jimmy. Very scared and very cold. Will you hold me?'

I sat up and held her for a long time. Her skin was cold against mine. Once she cried, but then she stopped. Every now and then she shivered quite violently. The rain splashed steadily outside. Cars passed and their lights swept my room too. Peep-peep-peep from the pedestrian crossing. I could hear lorries, then trains in the distance.

'It's late,' I said. 'And I have some work to do today. Tell me what happened.'

She didn't speak. I asked again but still she didn't speak. We sat like that for a long time. Some time later she grew limp and slept.

'So sleep. Sleep,' I said. 'I don't care . . . sleep. We'll talk later. I don't care.'

I disentangled my arms from her, and shifted so that I could sit on the edge of the bed. I was tired too. I took a blanket from the cupboard and went out to the sofa. Full daylight was outside the blinds now, and everyone had an engine to rev or a reason to shout. The milkman had special noisy bottles and passing girls had special noisy high heels. The blanket scratched my naked front and the creased leather of the old sofa stuck to my naked back. There's a beautiful girl in my bed and I'm sleeping out here with a newspaper over my face.

Saint Jimmy.

Chapter Twenty-seven

I was woken by the phone.

'You see the time?'

'I can see the time.' It was nine-thirty.

'Why aren't you here, Jim-boy?'

'I overslept.'

'Well, I'm out of business till you get here, and also I have to have my brother Rainer sitting here until you arrive, so will you please get up and get here.'

I got up. I went into the bedroom. Eleanor was – predictably – gone. I was pretty sure she'd be back. The sun was out. The light glowed through the slats of my blind as if the street was on fire. I snapped the blind open and rubbed the sleep from my eyes, blinded and bewildered by the intensity of the light behind the glass. The storm rainwater had cleaned the streets outside my flat at least of dust and staleness. Sodden dirt lay yet in grey clumps, clogging the gutters. But the people hadn't been washed away. My scruffy fellow citizens ambled along the street below my window. I washed and shaved, then dressed carefully in a grey suit and a red silk tie. I didn't want to be taken for an ambler.

I locked the front door and headed for the tube.

*

'This is my brother Rainer. And before you ask, yes he's my proper brother. Full brother.' Rainer was small and neatly built like Leon, but his skin was very light-coloured and his hair was tightly curled, honey colour. His eyes were grey. We were walking through the little yard to Leon's workshop and I was beginning to wish I'd worn old clothes or overalls. Squelch, squelch, the rain had fallen all over London. The mud crept up the sides of my shoes.

'Our grandfather was a German, and our father named Rainer after some German hero of his.'

'Rilke?'

Leon shook his head ruminatively. 'No ... definitely Rainer. It's all in the genes, you see. I got all the black ones, he got all the white ones. Our grandfather was a railway engineer, and Father was a mechanic. Rainer broke the tradition by joining the British army.'

'While you did your bit by joining a British jail.'

'Jim-boy. Life for a black man in Brixton, it criminalises him; you know?'

We went into the darkness of the workshop. It was under a railway viaduct and though there were neons overhead it took a few seconds to see clearly. The workshop was deserted of both cars and men, with just my Rover on a car lift.

'All you're doing is proving you read *New Society* while you were in there. What's going on here?'

'I gave my blokes the day off today, which is costing me a small fortune, Jim-boy. And my brother came up from Coulsden last night to look at your Rover.'

'Two mechanics for one little Rover?'

Leon hit a switch and arc-lamps shone on the underside of my car. Rainer stepped under the car. 'We have something to show you, Mr Jimbo.'

'Jenner, actually. Leon has taken it upon himself to call me Jim-*boy*. Jimmy will do.'

Rainer held his hand up. 'As you wish. For my part I am no car mechanic. I never have been. I run a nightclub.'

'Leon, why have you asked the Coulsden nightclub man here to stand under my car?'

Leon said nothing. Rainer grinned and beckoned me to join him. 'Mind your suit.' He twisted an arc-lamp so that it lit the gearbox area better and pointed at a cavity behind the prop shaft. 'Before I worked in nightclubs I was a soldier. I was in the RAOC.'

'What does that mean?'

'Bombs,' said Leon. He switched the lift on so the car rose six or so inches higher. 'He was a bombs expert.'

'And my brother found there something which made him call me. Something which looked like a bomb. So I came over from Coulsden and took a look.'

'And?'

'He's right. There was a bomb under your car. Just there, just where there's that rubber boot on the gearchange. I've taken it off.'

We went over to a workbench. 'Smell,' said Rainer. He held what looked like the innards of a portable wireless plus a couple of pounds of pink putty to my face. I sniffed.

'What do you get?'

'Marzipan. Commercial explosive.'

'Bang on. That's what it is. There's a mercury switch to set it off plus another switch which is activated by these, which I guess are components for a radio-controlled model aircraft or model car. It's not switched on, that part, so the state of the mercury switch doesn't matter. Once the radio-controlled part is switched on of course, it's a different matter. Then, the very next time you brake hard or accelerate hard, the mercury tips the glass phial . . . boom! There's only the rubber gaiter between the explosive and you and your front-seat passenger. Even a modest amount of explosive like this would kill you. It's not a particularly sophisticated device, but it'll do just nicely to blow you away exactly when somebody wants to. Boom.'

'Charming. Is it stable now?'

'I've taped up the contacts on the radio-controlled switch. The explosive is very fresh. Yes, it's stable. You'd have to take the tape off or short out the radio-controlled switch before the state of the mercury switch would matter.'

'And you don't think anyone's tried to arm it?'

Rainer shook his head and waited while a train passed above us. It sounded like thunder, only right in the room with us.

'I'm sure they haven't. And when they do one taped contact will close on another. Result . . . nothing. No circuit. Somewhere there is a man who thinks he has the drop on you, and my brother Leon here thinks that knowing that could be considerably to your advantage. He said we shouldn't call the police, we should get you to come and have a look-see.' Rainer smiled. 'We're not great callers of the police, anyway.'

'Good. Who do you think made it?'

'Impossible to say. Someone who knew what he was doing, but not a soldier, nothing like that. A classy villain who could get

130

his hands on some proper explosive, not some sodium chlorate rubbish. You haven't made any enemies in Ireland, have you?'

'Never been there... My ex-wife's got some Irish cousins, but even she don't hate me *that* much. This is someone who wants to get rid of me as and when he chooses. How far is the range of the radio control?'

'Not far if you want to be certain. Line of sight, really.'

Rainer and I walked out into the sunlight. The car lift whined as Leon let it down.

'No clues as to where it came from?' I asked.

'None. Totally innocuous. Japanese radio-control unit. English mercury switch. Italian explosive. Czech detonator. Perhaps the UN is trying to murder you.'

'I'll make the jokes about my life. What makes you say the explosive is Italian?'

'They colour it. Pink for military, green for civilian. They're the only ones who use it like that. I think you're going to have to call in the police if you want to do a really accurate trace on the components, and even *they* might have trouble tracking down the exact sources.'

'If I call the police they'll spend six months sodding around before they'd tell me just what you've told me. No, I don't want the police.'

Leon backed the car out of the garage and stood beside it with his bill. I got in and stuffed the bill in the dash.

'Thanks. I'll send you a cheque.'

'Jimmy, I don't want a cheque.'

'Well I don't have money now. You'll have to wait.'

Leon looked suitably despondent. Rainer gave me the bomb, plus the small plastic casing it had been mounted in.

'What are you going to do with it?' he asked.

'Dump it in the Thames. Thanks a lot, boys. I owe you one.'

'Well you can start paying it by wiping off our fingerprints before you do whatever you're going to do with it. You're not going to put it in the Thames.'

I turned the car. It was running sweetly. It always ran sweetly when Leon had it. A couple of days with me seemed to make all the difference. I tucked the bomb under the passenger seat of the Rover then did up my safety belt. Rainer stood by my open window.

'Why did you leave the army, Rainer?'

He shook his head.

131

'It's no good for boys like me. Seven years, I took. It's too long.'

'He beat up an RSM,' called Leon. 'Good and proper. He nearly killed him. He spent three of his seven years in prison.'

Rainer shrugged. 'Got to keep up the family tradition, eh?'

I put the car in 'drive'.

'Some tradition. Get your children to break with it.'

'What are you *really* going to do with it?'

He was frowning and serious.

'Telling you would make you an accessory. An aider and abettor. I don't want to do that to you two.'

'Well, be careful with it. Perhaps you'd better tell me.'

'For the moment nothing. When I find out who sent it I'm going to send it back . . . okay?'

'I hear nothing.'

Rainer turned his back and went over to join his brother. They were exactly alike, except one was dark and one pale. One wore overalls, the other casual clothes in the style of Marks and Spencer. Another suburban train roared above us. Kids peeked around the wooden gates to the yard. All the way home I was looking in my mirror for someone following me. I couldn't find anyone. I parked in Dalston, round the back of the police station where I expected not even the natives of Hackney would try to nick my car. I took a bus back up to Stoke Newington, then walked along to Defoe Mansions. The guided tour was outside, all staring slack-jawed at the newsagent's across the road from my flat. No doubt they were being told it was run by the Patel-Defoes, a sub-continental branch of the family.

I pushed through the tourists and went upstairs. No Eleanor and no message. Plenty of messages from George Tiler though, and one from Mavis Lasker – a status report on the still-disappeared Ronald Lasker, love of her life, support of her family, and I presume the only thing between her and living death with the kids on the dole in Northampton. The Sally Ann couldn't find him, the DHSS said 'Thanks very much for the information, don't call us we'll call you'. Mavis wanted to know what she should do. She was certain Ronald did not have the wherewithal to support himself any longer unless he had found work. It was clear she was worried about him. Just listening to Mavis made me tired, just thinking about her fate made me depressed. I rang George for preference, which is saying something.

'I've got a terrible problem, Jimmy. How soon can you get here?'

'What's the problem first?'

'Frames-Pargeter is coming up from Wiltshire to see me this very lunchtime.'

'And?'

'And my house is surrounded by police. I can't get out.'

'So let him come to you . . . what do you *mean* your house is surrounded? You sound as if you're under siege.'

'I feel as if I am. There's some major incident between here and Wapping tube, and they won't let anyone leave. Frames-Pargeter is supposed to be coming here and there's someone here who has to leave before he comes. But he can't.'

'He?'

'That's right.'

'George, what have you been up to?'

'*Nothing*. There's just this person here who can't get out and he really needs to before Tony Frames-Pargeter turns up otherwise we're going to have policemen's big boots tramping around my flat and all sorts of questions about 'How long have you been here?' and stuff like that with Tony Frames-Pargeter sitting there and listening to every word. I just can't afford it. Ple-ease, Jimmy. I'm sweating on it. You haven't much time.'

'Please what?'

'Please go to Wapping tube to head him off. Get a taxi down there and head him off for me. Otherwise he'll talk the police into letting him in and... can't you hurry?'

'I can hurry. Last time, though. These escapades of yours are getting silly. Is Eleanor there?'

'No. Of course not. She stayed with you. Hurry!'

'I'll hurry and I'll charge you but I won't *find* him. He'll take a taxi and come the other way or something.'

'Please, Jimmy. Just try.'

I rang off, then called another number.

'O'Keefe, please.' A click, then an electronic buzz.

'O'Keefe.'

'It's Jenner.'

'Jimmy! Good to hear you. How are you?'

'Not bad. How's the insurance business keeping you?'

'Nicely. Even if I say so myself. I saw your wife the other day.'

'Not now, Denis. I'm in a rotten rush.'

'What do you want?'

'I want to know how all those old contacts of yours in the police are. I need some information and I don't think anyone is going to just give it to me.'

'What?'

'Bloke called Bianchi, Paolo Bianchi. Aged around, oh I don't know, sixty, early sixties. Grey hair, slim, well dressed. Lives in Chelsea but I don't know the address. I believe he's actually domiciled here in England. That's the impression I got.'

'What do you want to know about him?'

'Everything. Absolutely everything. Could you find out?'

'I don't need to find out and I don't need to ask any old contacts, Jimmy. Bianchi is famous. He's the Italian Snow King.'

'Snow King?'

'That's right. He is Mr Import-Export Colombian Snow for Italy, only the Italian government doesn't like that business going on so he's come here. I mean, Jimmy, there are Italian warrants on that guy stacked about a foot high, and he's living here very openly. As long as he stays in England, he's okay. We're in love with due process, so he gets to stay. The Italians have wanted that bastard for years, even before I left the job, but they never get him.'

'What happens?'

'People put their names to affidavits, then fall off cliffs or go on holiday and get eaten by sharks or run down by cars or something like that. What have you got to do with this man?'

'Is he a Mafia man?'

There was a silence. Then Denis said, 'What do you think, Jim? I mean it's not the De La Salles or the Jesuits who are doing all this. Mr Bianchi is a very nasty piece of work and if you have anything on him I suggest you turn it over to our former colleagues at once.'

'Preferably via *you* so you can get credit with all those detectives you keep tapping for information.'

'On behalf of people like you, Jimmy. I tap them on behalf of boys like you and me. They scratch my back, I've got to scratch theirs.'

'You're going to be busy, then. Are you sure they don't help because they get a good drink out of it?'

'Jimmy! I am shocked indeed. The very idea.'

'Of course. Could Bianchi be the sort of bloke who'd use a bomb?'

'Not personally, but he'd certainly arrange one for you, if

that's what you've got in mind. Are you thinking of going round and asking him to bomb someone?'

'No. I've got to go now. I've got to do something.'

'Meet me and tell me what you've got.'

'Later.'

'Tonight.'

'No.'

'Tell me now then.'

'No. I've really got to go. I mean it.'

'I'll give you the low-down on this Bianchi.'

'You mean I'll give you. You stick to solving insurance frauds, Sherlock. And thanks a lot.'

I went downstairs to look for a taxi. Some hopes.

*

'I despair of him sometimes,' Tony Frames-Pargeter said, running his fingers through his hair and wrinkling up his red, drinker's nose. 'The fact is, he can be really bloody stupid. What's today's excuse, another of his "friends" being difficult?'

'I don't know about that, Mr Pargeter. The reason he had me meet you was absolutely A1 gen, as you could see for yourself.'

We were in a taxi, heading for the city. The taxi had a cricket score on its meter, owing to me having sat outside Wapping tube station in it for fifteen minutes. The street next to the tube was taped off with white plastic tape that said MP, MP, MP, MP all the way along it, interspersed with little blue crowns. Further along the street a line of bobbies in blue denim were crawling along the ground, like Muslims at prayer only shuffling forward. Tony Frames-Pargeter had turned up in a taxi which stopped next to the tube station simply because it couldn't take him past the 'MP' tape.

'Jenner . . .'

'Jimmy, please,' I said, through gritted teeth.

'I don't give a shit about his chums. The fact that George is a misogynist will only ever cause trouble because he has himself contrived to make it do so. Oh yes, we all know about that. I've given him enough broad hints that it's no disqualification in itself. I told him outright at his house the other day, when you were there. I mean, if being queer barred you from being an MP there'd be no bastards to form a government. He just doesn't *listen.*'

135

'MP?' I was still thinking of the tapes across the road, MP – Metropolitan Police.

'Member of Parliament. Ours is just about to retire and we approached George about taking it on. He's ideal, he owns land in the constituency, he's young, personable.'

'Young-*ish*.'

'He'd be a dream with all the old ladies in the constituency. There are very few architects in parliament and none on our side. He's flexible and intelligent. He's quite a star in a way . . . but he keeps running round like a lunatic trying to hide his past. I even had some greasy little sod come to me the other day trying to flog bloody love letters George had written him.'

The taxi rounded a corner and Tony Frames-Pargeter leaned confidentially towards me. By the smell of him I should have said the gin bottle on the Swindon to Paddington train needed replacing.

'Can you imagine that, Jenner?'

'Yes. Gilligan?'

'I don't know his name. He looked typical . . . which of course old George does not. I sent him away with a flea in his hear. "Fuck off, you little skunk!" I told him.'

'Please . . . the driver.'

Frames-Pargeter nodded slowly. 'You're right. Don't want to say too much in front of him. Probably a fucking socialist.' He laughed.

'This'll do.'

We were in Lower Thames Street. The taxi stopped and I handed over most of the contents of my wallet. We walked along a narrow alley. The boom of the traffic receded. At the end was a tiny doorway into a riverside pub. The balcony over the river was packed with City types and their girls, secretaries with padded bras and wiggly walks. The bar was nearly empty, though.

'Let me get this straight,' I said. 'You're saying that George is a prospective Member of Parliament?'

''S right. Mum's the word, though. Till old Sir Henry, our incumbent, actually tips the world off to his plans.'

'Mum's the word. Here.' I gave him his gin and tonic and we went to a corner of the room. Fake beams hung above my head, draped with mass-produced horse brasses. A scroll, artificially aged paper, announced in hand-drawn Gothic that King Charles had had a pint with Nell Gwyn here once.

'So George has been panicking about his past? Hence he hired me?'

'Bloody stupid,' Frames-Pargeter said loudly.

'Quite. But I think you'd better have a frank discussion with him soon. Give him a ring. At the moment he's stuck inside his flat because of that police performance you saw. He's got some friend with him and the person can't get out. He'll get out soon, Tony, and I think you should go round there and explain to George Tiler in words of one syllable what's what, because George has got it round his neck. And he certainly doesn't know *you* know.'

He nodded. 'Okay. I'll do just that.'

'What did the man who came to see you look like?'

Frames-Pargeter stood. 'Let me buy a drink first and I'll tell you.'

The doorway to the balcony opened and a young man came in with empty glasses for filling. I caught a glimpse of the river, dull grey with glints of light on it. A girl laughed. The barman sang a boisterous 'Yes, sir!' A man opposite me was reading the first edition of the *Standard*. Wapping Bloodbath – Police Seek Man.

Chapter Twenty-eight

Back in Stoke Newington, I had deflected Tony Frames-Pargeter from visiting George Tiler's and I was exhausted. This politics business calls for men with a stronger constitution than mine. Too little sleep and consecutive days of daytime drinking had made me feel weak and useless, more than ready to lie down for an hour or two of the afternoon and pass responsibility for life to the rest of the world for a while. You worry, I need a rest.

I was a hundred and fifty yards from my flat when a kid stopped me right there at the street corner. He was one of last night's revellers outside Defoe Mansions. The runt. He was wearing a black nylon tracksuit with yellow, green and red stripes down the sides of the legs, he was wearing a beanie-hat with about a hundredweight of hair stuffed inside and he was drinking Red Stripe Crucial Brew from a can, lifting, sipping, speaking. The runt was looking pleased with himself.

'There's coppers down there looking for you, mate,' he said. 'They was asking everyone which flat was yours. Old geezer with grey hair was asking.'

'How did you know he was a copper?'

'You can tell, you know?' He smiled pleasantly, probably happy that someone else had trouble with the law for a change.

'What did you tell them?'

Sip. 'Nothing. No one did. They was just looking for a geezer that lived there who had a walking-stick. Young geezer with a walking-stick. That's you. No one else like that round here. No one young.'

'Cheers.' I went to walk past him.

'Hang on. Ain't you that private detective geezer?'

'Maybe.' He was standing in my way. 'Maybe not.'

'You are then.' He scratched his head under his beanie. 'Ain't the information worth anything to you?'

'No. How old are you?'

He pulled himself up to full height, about five-four.

'Eighteen.'

'Leave off.'

'Sixteen, then.'

'You're lucky if you're thirteen and you're a cheeky little sod . . . what's your name?'

'Graham.' He sipped at the lager can again.

'Well, I should hide that, Graham, before the coppers see you, otherwise you'll get arrested. I'm quite certain they'll arrest you and put you in care if they find you slugging that stuff.'

'You're the one who's gonna get arrested.' He slugged from the can this time, lifting it high and draining it. 'Less than ten minutes, I reckon, unless you walk the other way. Come on. It's worth something to you.' He looked at a group of kids on the other side of the road, observing us.

'Maybe. Or maybe you're winding me up to score points with your pals over there . . . what d'you say?'

'I say there's a load of coppers hanging round your house and that nice young white girl you was in there with last night took one look at them and made off about, oh, quarter of an hour ago. I say they're going to arrest you. I say. How much is it worth?'

'Tomorrow.'

'How much?'

'*Tomorrow.*'

I walked on. Across the road Graham's pals were laughing at him. Obviously the trick was to get money from me. Graham had failed. Go back to school, Graham.

*

There was a young man filling a telephone box, almost bursting out of it, a few yards along from my flat. He was a big boy and the telephone box designers hadn't had him in mind at all. He wasn't making a call. There were two more large young men sitting in a Ford Granada at the corner of the street. The car had two aerials and was on a double yellow line. They didn't look all that bothered about the parking regulations or meter maids. I

139

pushed the button on the pedestrian crossing and waited for the 'peep-peep-peep'. You peeped for her, now peep for me. A hand touched my elbow.

'Jimmy. Jimmy Jenner. Long time, eh? Good to see you, Jimmy.'

Detective Chief Superintendent Maher of the East London Murder Squad smiled at me as if he meant it. Maybe he did.

'Good to see you too, Mr Maher. What age do they retire you blokes at? I'd have thought you'd be double-digging an allotment by now.'

'Oh Jimmy!' His face was full of mock anguish. 'That's not fair . . . that's not fair at all. I've a long time yet. Are you on your way up to your flat?'

'I am.'

'Well, I was wondering if we might have a chat.' He waved some envelopes before me. 'I took the liberty of picking up your post. Are those your keys?'

By the time you get to Maher's age and rank the only reason for coming out to pick up mugs like me is that you enjoy doing it. It's your hobby. I smiled sheepishly, handed over the keys and followed Maher to the badly parked Ford Granada. By this time the two young men were standing at the side of it, scratching their left armpits. The fellow from the phone box followed Maher and myself, scratching his armpit too.

'I hope those mad-looking buggers aren't as trigger-happy as they look, Mr Maher, because they're making me nervous. I've got nothing more dangerous in my pocket than a packet of Wrigley's and a five-pound note.'

'Take no notice,' said Maher. He threw the man from the telephone box my keys. 'They're a bit excitable. They're young. Ignore it.'

'Well it's not *you* they'll be aiming at.'

'Sit down, sit down,' he said in a schoolteachery voice to the two young men by the car. The young men didn't sit until I did. I slid into the back seat of the Ford with Maher and he passed my stick to the young man in the passenger seat. The young man twisted the stick as if it was a swordstick or had a rifle hidden in it or something. We drove quickly away. The runt stood at the kerbside shaking his head and laughing at me as we drove past. In the front of the car the radio spoke with a burst of excitement, spoke something unintelligible. Maher wound down his window.

140

'It's hot in here, isn't it, Jimmy?'

I didn't answer.

At the Balls Pond Road we stopped and Maher and me swapped into the back of a marked Transit van driven by one uniform policeman. The large men in the Granada were polishing their sunglasses and trying to look as if they weren't policemen. Why else would three big men in suits drive around in a Ford Granada with two aerials?

'I need my stick,' I said. Maher nodded to the Transit driver, who went to fetch it. Maher and me were left alone.

'I take it this is not about a trip to Gibraltar?' I said.

'What about Gibraltar?'

'Judy wants to go to Spain. You remember Spain? She was wondering if going via Gib would be okay.'

Maher shrugged. 'Do what you want.'

The Transit driver came back and handed Maher my stick before sliding behind the wheel and starting the van. Maher gave the stick to me.

'This means you don't think I'm some dangerous master criminal with a swordstick, a black cape and a vow to kill or be killed?'

'Don't be silly. Just relax.' The Transit lurched forward. I grabbed the seatback to save myself falling. Maher grinned. 'Relax a *bit*, Jimmy. Don't go all floppy.'

*

Eamon Maher was in his early fifties. Very trim, with blue eyes and grey, almost white, hair and a nice line in dapper grey suits. We were sitting in a traffic jam in Dalston. There's always a traffic jam in Dalston. I could see the police station down the road, and knew my guilty car was sitting behind it, bomb under the passenger seat. Maher pulled a plastic bag out of his side pocket.

'Seen this before?'

It was a sheet of paper with destinations, numbers and prices written on it.

I cleared my throat.

'Yes. I've seen it. How did you come by it?'

'One of our scene-of-crime blokes found it on the floor of a rented car early this morning. Unfortunately, Jimmy, inside the rented car was the body of a woman, plus a badly injured man. Both shot through the head at close range.'

'Where was the car?'

'Wapping. Down by the waterside, by those big warehouses that are being ponced up.'

'Any idea who the people are?'

'None. I'm counting on you to help, there. We've got no papers, no ID at all. Just a man in a suit and a woman sitting next to him with her brains blown out. Your piece of paper was on the floor . . . that was the only document in the car. Even the rental docs were gone, we had to trace the motor off the number plates. Hot, isn't it?' He struggled with the Transit's sliding window.

'You said that in the other car.'

Maher frowned. 'That's because it is, James. I speak the truth. I hope you do too. Who's the man?'

'I haven't seen him. Describe him.'

Maher shook his head. 'I haven't seen him either. He's in the London Hospital. All I've got is a middle-aged man, grey hair, wears a suit, got a hole in his face.'

'It could be you.'

'*Extra* hole, smartie pants. In the side, too.'

'Why isn't he dead?'

'Thick skull and very good luck, according to the quacks. Maybe he will be dead soon. It's too hot, Jimmy. These vans aren't meant for hot weather. It's an oven.' The traffic moved forward again.

'It's the weather,' I said. 'Who rented the motor?'

'Someone who doesn't exist. We've already been through all that. Very early this morning.' He yawned. 'It rained all night, did you know that?'

'Not all night.'

'You were about then?'

'I was awake. I couldn't sleep . . . when exactly was the car found, Mr Maher?'

'I'll be the detective, don't you think? Nice suit you're wearing. Silk tie, too. I've never seen you dressed up like this before. Do you think it's the day for a grey worsted, though?'

'Thanks for the advice.' We were outside the police station now, and past it. 'Where are you taking me?'

'To have a look at the dead bint, Jimmy. See if you can give us a clue who's who and what's what.'

I took the plastic bag containing my bill to Charles Wallace and held it between finger and thumb. I was thinking of Eleanor.

'Was the woman very young?'

'Yes. Wait till you see them. Then you can say.'

'Fat, thin? Dark, blonde? Old or young? How old?'

'Thin, twenty-ish, dark. Okay? Do you mind if we have a look round your flat?'

'I thought you were already doing it.'

The driver put the sirens on and turned right into Queensbridge Road against the traffic, against the rules. Maher pushed at the sliding window again. 'Air at last. Is this a bit better or what?'

We sped between the vertical ghettos of tower blocks. Kids played in the roadside dirt. Dusty cars were parked there too, some broken down, some dumped. This corpse-and-copper caper was getting a bit too common for my taste, I thought. I don't like going to mortuaries and I don't like watching life from the back of a police van. Maher was sweating but steadfastly refusing to loosen his tie. We turned left into Hackney Road, then right into Warner Place and Squirries Street.

'Are we going to the London Hospital?' I said. 'Are we going to see the man?'

'No. We're going to the mortuary, Jimmy. So you can give me a considered opinion about this dead bird. And I wouldn't be in the least surprised if we ended up in the Murder Squad office in Peter Street nick. Who is the man?'

'I don't know. I haven't seen him.'

If the uniformed driver hadn't been there Maher would loosen his tie. Or take his jacket off even, I thought. A man with too strong a sense of status. 'Do you think you recognise the woman from the description?'

'I don't know. Maybe . . . I haven't seen . . .'

'Hey!' Maher called. The driver swung the van across Bethnal Green Road with a blast on the siren.

'What's up?' Maher called.

'Sorry, sir. I thought we were in a hurry.'

We clattered across a cobbled surface, then under a deafening railway arch. The siren was still on and the sound bounced back into us from the sooty walls of the long arch. I could see the reflections of our flashing blue light, too. Then we were back in daylight and cars were diving to the kerb to let us past.

143

'Slow down,' said Maher. 'She's already dead.'

'How about seeing the bloke first?' I asked.

'You young fellows are all short of patience. Just be patient. All in good time. Unless you've had a previously undisclosed career as a brain-surgeon you won't be any use to this fellow we found.'

He took my bill to Charlie Wallace from my hand and put it back in his side pocket.

'How do you know that was from me?'

'I didn't know. I guessed. There was just something funny about the writing. Something that rang a bell. I felt as if I recognised it. So I looked at the dates, and the kind of things being charged for, and I thought, "What kind of man would have written this?" Eventually I decided it was a salesman or something. A representative. I wondered what the man did that he had representatives who sent him personal bills. I still don't know that . . . what does he do?'

'If it's the man I wrote the bill for, he's an actor, an Englishman domiciled in the USA. Called Charles Wallace.'

'Oh . . . Charlie Wallace! "Butler" fellow during the fifties? That's the fellow okay, now I know who it is.'

'I think he is well known for playing butler parts. I was looking for his daughter, a girl called Eleanor. It's a long story, Mr Maher. I'll tell you.'

'Won't you just?'

'How did you get from there to me? From a representative to me?'

'Easily. A private investigator is one type of representative. You're a private investigator. The handwriting looked like yours, I realised. So I rang your wife and said, "I have a bill for some work in Paris, Sergeant Jenner, which your husband might have done. Do you know whether he has been in France recently?"'

'And?'

'And she, good loyal soul that she is, said that she was no longer your wife and had never considered herself to be your keeper and that where you went and what you did was no longer any of her concern.'

'Good old Judy.'

'Good old Judy indeed. I presumed from the fact that she didn't answer directly that the real answer to my question was "yes". So I could presume from that that you had worked for at least one of the poor people we found in that car today, Jimmy Jenner, and that I had a duty to talk to you. I could also presume that there were ruthless people involved here, and that they might have an eye on you, or even someone with you. So I decided that I'd better come properly prepared in case there were any... any *difficulties*. In case the person who'd done that shooting was with you or near you.'

'Every kid in the street knew you were policemen.'

'That bad?' Maher stroked his chin. 'I'm disappointed.'

''Fraid so.'

'Oh well. I've been honest with you, Jimmy, and obviously this is going to be quite a difficult time we're just going into, so I want you to be honest with me. Okay? I want absolute frankness from you, otherwise we're not going to get anywhere.'

'I can make a guess who the woman is now.'

'Don't guess now. We're nearly there. Wait until you've seen her, tell me who she is, then tell me all you know... everything. This is a vicious murder, Jimmy, and I can't be doing with any evasiveness on it. Any of that stuff, well, I expect we'd be forced to make charges.' He smiled and slapped me on the shoulder. 'Not that I expect it to come to that. We're old friends, aren't we? Well, I feel as if we are, anyway.'

I nodded. This was the point Maher wanted to arrive at, this was why he'd come to fetch me personally and why he'd made the journey alone with me in the back of the police Transit. He wanted to be my friend, my pal. He wanted to be close to me and trusted by me. Maher was a subtle man, and didn't need rough stuff or histrionics of any sort to get what he wanted. All he had to do was convince people that his side was their side. Convince *me*. Then I would tell him everything I knew, every little detail. That's what 'honest' meant to Eamon Maher. I would tell him everything, he would tell me nothing. That's the deal.

'Absolutely honest, Jimmy. Straight down the line.'

I nodded.

'Okay. What do you want to know?'

'See the dead bird first. Presuming you can, tell me who she is, then tell me why you think she's dead. You know... an honest assessment.'

I nodded again. I *was* honest with him too. Well, nearly. But not all at once, and I didn't start right then. Up ahead the traffic into Whitechapel Road was jammed, and the driver put the sirens on again, effectively drowning conversation. We were in the oncoming lane of what was only a two-lane road, and the driver swung us left at the traffic lights, towards Mile End, towards the London Hospital, with screeching tyres and scattered pedestrians. I held tight to the seatback. Maher called, 'Already dead. Already dead.' The driver turned the sirens off again.

'From bullets in the head,' I said.

'Very funny. Make that the last joke about this, please, because I've got this case, Jimmy, and it's a big problem for me. Is it a gang thing?'

'I don't believe so.'

The van drew into the side of the hospital, down a ramp to the mortuary entrance. The entrance was subterranean, with a deck of concrete above it. In the gloom I could make out the faces of some men by the double doors. A cigarette glowed.

Maher said, 'Mortuary. I take it you've been in one before. I mean we don't want you going all loose at the knees and spewing on us.'

One of Maher's minions opened the double doors for us. Yellow electric light flowed out. The floor was polished linoleum, thick and squeaky. And there was that smell, that indefinable smell somewhere between ether and dust, age and antiseptic.

'Oh, I've been in one before,' I said.

Chapter Twenty-nine

Heathrow doesn't belong to London or even England. Heathrow is part of the airport community of the world, with a homogenised atmosphere, with electronic bulletin boards, with multilingual 'bing-bong' announcements. Heathrow has hundreds of bemused people guarding bags while others go off in search of a telephone, lavatory, information. A relative. In the midst of all this me and DCS Eamon Maher were sitting on a black vinyl sofa. We were waiting. A uniformed inspector came over to us.

'Mr Maher?'

We followed him to a door marked 'Staff Only', then down a corridor, then into a room off the corridor. The room had a mixture of easy chairs of the same pattern as the sofas in the main terminal hall, small tables and plastic stacking chairs. One wall in the room was of glass, a one-way mirror, approximately twenty feet long and twelve feet deep. The mirror stretched from the ceiling to below our floor level, and was made safe by a guardrail of hardwood stretching all across the front of it. The room must once have been an observation balcony, and had since been glassed in with the one-way mirror to give the observers privacy. A row of black easy chairs was lined up in front of the glass and at the far end of the line two uniformed Customs and Excise men were staring through the glass, occasionally making notes on clipboards they held on their laps.

'Policemen,' the uniformed inspector said to the Customs men, by way of explanation. 'I'm going to leave them here.'

The Customs men nodded assent and the uniformed inspector

147

pointed to a phone on the wall. 'Direct line to my office, sir. Just call me when you want me.'

'Thank you. We'll call.'

'Coffee?' said the uniformed man to Maher.

'Coffee,' said Maher. 'Coffee would be very good indeed. Milk no sugar, twice.'

We sat and the policeman left. On the other side of the glass people were gathering their luggage from a carousel, then streaming through a concourse and choosing red-channel/green-channel. The Customs men further along the row of seats smiled and nodded at us, then resumed taking notes. They didn't speak to each other.

'Denis O'Keefe tells me Bianchi is the Italian Snow King.'

'Maybe he is. What does Denis know? He's been out of the job for a year.'

'I thought we were going to be honest with each other. I can't help that girl if you're not honest with me, Mr Maher.'

'You don't have to help her. It's our problem now...' He stretched and yawned. 'But I'll tell you about Bianchi. He *was* a major figure in organised crime both in Italy and the United States, and that means by inference here... I mean that anyone with his sort of background who turned up here would get a polite audience from the people running things. Who that was, would, of course, depend on when he turned up.

'Back to the beginning. Bianchi was born in Palermo in 1922, one of a long line of urban criminals. He is not some peasant turned into a poacher by unhappy circumstances. It's his family business. By the start of the Second World War he was in the United States as a "refugee" from the fascists... it makes you smile, doesn't it? His father was a very well-known Mafia man, so they get into the US as "refugee union organiser and family". By the end of the Second World War the father is dead owing to him having a fatal misunderstanding with a bullet. The son is all adrift in New York, neither being a born member of one of the American Mafia families nor able to muscle his way in from the outside. Paolo Bianchi is just another Italian hooligan.

'Now, Jimmy, I can't account for the difference, but by 1952, by the time he is thirty, he is nothing of the sort. He is an important man in New York City and if you want to buy South American stuff, Bianchi is the man you have to go to because he has the connections. He's not the head of one of these so-called Mafia families, not even close to being one... he's just the man

148

with all the connections. Eventually, by a mixture of the FBI and the American taxman taking a fancy to him, plus burgeoning opportunities presenting themselves in his native Italy, Mr Bianchi makes his way home to Italy. He's rich and he reckons he's going to get richer by supplying all the silly bastards in Europe with the same rubbish as all the silly bastards in America are taking.'

'Did it work?'

'Sort of. At first, yes. But there were problems. All the Italians already in Italy didn't see why they had to do business with this outsider. Of course, Bianchi and his backers from New York and Palermo soon managed to bridge his credibility gap to the satisfaction of all the boys in Milan and similar points north, and they did so by the usual and usually expedient methods of shooting everyone who disagreed with them.'

'Bianchi organised this?'

'No. His backers did. And they did it so well that by 1960 Paolo Bianchi had replaced his former career of being the man in New York you had to see to buy South American drugs with a career of being the man you had to see in Milan to buy South American drugs. *I* first met him, Jimmy, some fifteen years after that, in London. Then he was in the full flow of his career. *Then* he was the Italian Snow King, as O'Keefe calls it.'

'You met him?'

'Yes. I was a DCI on Drugs Squad. I met him in a terraced house in Peckham, overlooking the Rye. He'd come here to escape the attentions of the Italian judiciary, in particular one man in the Italian Ministry of Justice, a socialist MP who'd got the job as one of those deals they have to do there if they ever want to form a government. The MP is . . . *was*, a brilliant anti-drugs campaigner, former academic, was a real star for the future . . .'

'Called Di Nemico. Used to work in Paris as a university lecturer. Was until recently a Minister of Justice under the last or the-one-before-that Italian government? Is now deceased.'

'The same. Very ambitious, and he'd got his teeth into Paolo Bianchi in 1975, just as I said, and he wasn't letting go. Who could blame him?'

'So what was Bianchi to you?'

'Well, he had the right to live here because we'd recently acceded to the Treaty of Rome. There was nothing anyone in Britain could do to force Bianchi to leave unless the Italians could get the required stuff together to get an extradition order in the normal way. Of course, they couldn't manage it. You can imagine, every time someone gives a statement, they meet with an accident. It's only in the last few years the Italians have even started to get on top of this problem. Back in 1975, they were nowhere.'

The coffee came, brought by a surly constable who clearly didn't think much of being asked to act as a waiter for another policeman, whatever the rank. As the uniformed constable put the cups beside us I saw his colleague in the doorway waiting to go on patrol. He held a machine-gun. Maher caught my eye.

'I don't suppose any of us will get used to seeing coppers carrying machine-guns, Jimmy. Don't worry.'

'Worry isn't the point.'

Maher smiled a friendly smile, a father confessor's smile designed to put me at ease. 'As long as we're unhappy that someone has to have one I'm sure we'll have nothing to fear.'

'Sophism. Save it for news cameras and politicians. The issue is Di Nemico. Di Nemico is alive and well in 1975 and he's looking at a great career in government. All he needs is a coup. His coup, I guess you are telling me, is to run old Paolo Bianchi out of town.'

'Not out of town. Into jail. At least that's what he wanted. He had a pet investigating magistrate called ... called, oh I don't know. But anyway these two were the hottest game around, they're both as smart as each other and they're both determined to break Bianchi and for that matter anyone who has it in mind to replace him. Italy is going to be finished as a drugs importing point for the rest of Europe and these two heroes would have medals on their chests to prove that they were the men who broke this menace and put the moving force, Bianchi, in prison. Only Bianchi skipped to England, the government fell and was rebuilt a couple of times in Italy, the investigating magistrate goes to Finland for his holiday and doesn't take his *carabinieri* guards with him. Of course, he didn't make it as far as Bolzano before his car blew up.'

'Radio controlled with a mercury switch, placed under the gearchange tunnel?'

'I don't know . . . why do you ask?'

'Just asking.'

'*Medori.* Giuseppe Medori is the name of the magistrate. I remember it now. Medori died, the government changed a few

150

times, Di Nemico had a couple of new jobs instead, suddenly the whole thing ran out of steam. Bianchi was here, not in Italy . . . you know.'

'But Di Nemico kept after him, later, when he was Minister of Justice. Is that what happened?'

'Sort of.'

Maher sipped his coffee and stared through the glass screen. Another mob was milling around the carousel. The Customs men were taking notes again.

'None of which,' I said, 'explains what you were doing in Bianchi's house in Peckham. Even if you were doing Di Nemico's work, you wouldn't do it from Bianchi's front room.'

Another sip of coffee, another stare through the glass screen. Maher sighed.

'It's not that simple. This is very difficult, what I'm going to tell you next, and you can't divulge it. Absolutely secret. Do I have your word?'

'Yes. Okay.'

'Even other policemen. You can't even tell other policemen about it. Especially those Frogs.'

'You have my word.'

Maher drained his cup.

'You see, Jimmy, at first the Italians really wanted him, and really wanted to prosecute him. But then Bianchi became very useful both to the Americans and ourselves, and then we had to persuade the Italians that they only had to make out that they wanted him, please, while we were making use of him. That was very difficult, but eventually they agreed. It would have been very difficult to reconstruct the case after Medori was killed, anyway. I mean, they have half the witnesses pushing up daisies and now the investigating magistrate, too. We convinced them that they stood to gain by playing along with us.'

'Let me get this straight, you convinced the Italian authorities to ease off on a well-known major drugs importer and he got to keep the money, and the lifestyle and his reputation and all the rest of it on the strength of him co-operating with you?'

'More precisely with the Americans. Ours was a sideshow, simply because he was here.'

'And were witnesses still getting murdered during this play-acting?'

'What do you take us for?' Maher seemed genuinely shocked.

'And he lived in peace in England ever since? And he still

does, with friends who are politicians and all that and pretty girls hanging on his arms and a great big Merc to drive around in and a chauffeur to drive it? I mean, who says crime doesn't pay? He got to keep all that on the strength of turning in a few errant Yanks. We're in the wrong business, Mr Maher. Who said all this was okay, I mean in England?'

'I can't say. You know I've broken the law by even telling you this much, Jimmy. He's not active, at least we can be comforted by that, and quite a number, not just a few, of the Americans he put the finger on are doing porridge. That's the best we can ever hope for.'

One of the Customs men sitting along from us picked up a walkie-talkie by his side and said, 'Got him. Blue suit, going into the green channel now. Can you see him?'

The radio squawked back at him. Below us a man in a blue suit walked nonchalantly into the green Customs channel. He held a briefcase and a light suitcase and looked like he might have been a salesman. The Customs man said into the radio, 'Here's the second. She's wearing a floral-print dress. Just entering now.'

A middle-aged woman walked into the green channel too. She looked like everybody's Mum. The two Customs men next to us stood and stretched. They were exhilarated. The one nearest was very young and sported a beard to give him authority. He said to Maher and me, 'Drugs. They send them in twos, so we get so excited with the first we miss the second. It's a rotten trick on the couriers, of course.'

'How did you know?' I said.

'Information.'

He nodded and his colleague nodded to emphasise the value of information, as if there was something special in the very word. *Information.*

'Bye then.' They left.

'Here's ours,' I said. Letellier walked into the luggage-reclaiming hall. He looked every bit the Frenchman, suddenly. His suit was cut so as to imply a swagger when he walked. His hair was neat, close cropped. He had his detective's issue raincoat draped over his shoulder and he looked as if he found it all rather boring. Maher picked up the phone.

'Chief Superintendent Maher here. Our man's down in the Customs hall now.'

A few seconds later the uniformed inspector came out of a

door to the Customs hall. There was no handle on the hall-side of the door, so he left it slightly ajar. He touched Letellier on the elbow and led him back through the doorway.

Maher yawned and stretched.

'You see, Jimmy? Every flight there's some creep trying to bring more of the stuff in. Two on that flight alone, even with your Paris police friend aboard. We have to do whatever we can to stop it. And if that means back-pedalling on one chap so that we can clean up a whole ring of them . . . well, there's hardly any choice, is there?'

'Did Di Nemico back-pedal too? Was he in on it?'

'I don't know. I really don't know. I presume he was. Your French pal should be able to tell us, surely, whether Di Nemico was shot for this reason or that. It's not my problem at the moment.'

'What is?'

'Dead women in Wapping. Film stars spouting blood in the London Hospital. Can't you read the headlines now?'

'He's not spouting blood or anything else. And he's nobody's idea of a film star. He's a bit-part actor.'

Maher opened the door and stood back for me to pass through first.

'Didn't you read his book *In the Can*? It was all the rage a few months ago. All the dirt, Hollywood and London both. You should have read it, Jimmy . . . well, probably you're the wrong generation. For my age group, well all that stuff matters. We were more innocent in those days. His book was a revelation.'

'You'll make me cry. Who was buying Bianchi's coke in the early fifties? My generation was still on Welfare Service orange juice.'

'You're a very bitter man, Jimmy. Come on, let's cop this Frog before the boys downstairs start frisking him and looking closely at his passport.'

Chapter Thirty

When we left the mortuary a second time Letellier was ashen-faced. We walked along a neon-lit corridor, then into a medical conference room. The room was furnished in the NHS utility style, with uncomfortable plastic 'stacking' chairs of brilliant orange and a veneered wood table in the centre of the room. Venetian blinds were drawn. I pushed two slats apart to look at the night outside. A yard, parked cars; one white-coated man walked across. I couldn't hear his footsteps. The window was sealed double-glazing. I could hear Letellier, though.

Letellier had sat at the veneered table with a uniformed sergeant; the Coroner's Officer. On either side of them, as if they were a bridge four, were Maher and another senior detective. Maher didn't bother introducing the other detective, but the man's manner was of one who was used to giving orders.

Letellier gave a statement to the Coroner's Officer. The dead girl was called Marie Renan, yes, she was in the employ of the French government, yes Letellier was familiar with her. No, he was not her immediate superior, no he would not specify what her job had been. Letellier's accent was very marked in London. In Paris he'd seemed to speak perfect colloquial English. Not now.

Marie Renan was twenty-six. No, Letellier could not say what she had been doing in London. He wrote down her address. He signed the statement. Maher thanked the uniformed sergeant and told him he could leave. Then they were quite silent for a long time, and the double-glazing sealed off the world outside. Maher turned on an Anglepoise, switched off the main light, then said to Letellier, 'I want to get this straight. Off the record. Policeman to policeman. This girl Renan was yours, right?'

Letellier nodded.

'And she was here posing as an American tourist and following him.' He jerked his thumb towards me.

Letellier nodded again.

Maher raised an eyebrow. His companion, a large, ruddy-faced man who might have been a farmer, raised an eyebrow too.

'Why?' said Maher.

'Because he was a suspect in a serious crime in Paris.' Letellier shrugged. 'It's normal.'

'Not *here* it isn't, chummy. Follow who you want in France, but here it is not normal for French police to follow the citizenry around.'

'What?'

Maher ignored him. 'The girl was a police officer?'

Letellier nodded again.

'And you set her to wandering around England trailing this flyblown bloody fantasist on the basis he might lead you to whoever had committed this serious crime in Paris?'

Letellier gave no reply.

'She was following *him*. Yes?' The thumb again.

'Yes.'

'You asked her to. Yes?'

'Yes. To follow.'

Another long pause.

'What was the crime? What crime was Jenner here a suspect in?'

'A murder.'

'A murder.' Maher looked at the ruddy-faced detective and said again, 'A murder.' Then to Letellier, 'Anyone in particular?'

'We believe the dead one was a man called Paolo Bianchi. Half-English, half-Italian. Jenner was there around the time the man was killed. He was . . . uh, evasive when we spoke to him, but there was reason to suppose he had some involvement with the uh, event. So I released him and had him followed.'

'But she wasn't following him when she was shot, was she? She was in a car parked down a dark street with this Charles Wallace character. I don't suppose she was following Jenner then, do you?'

155

'I don't know.'

'Jenner says he wasn't there. So while your ace girl detective is blundering around London looking for Jenner here – who is, by the way, tucked up in bed all the time with only his false leg for company – she picks up this actor bloke, decides she'd much rather be with him than Jenner and has just taken him down some dark street in Wapping to give him a blow-job or tell him his fortune or what, when out of the shadows steps someone with a pistol. Bang bang bang, brains on the dashboard. Famous actor lying half out the car with whatever wits he ever had draining out of his bonce and on to the cobbles. Have you got the scenario?'

'No.'

He wasn't meant to. Maher was in a fury. 'Do you speak French, Jenner?'

'Not much.'

'How about you, Mr Roberts? What's French for "You're a pillock?"'

Mr Roberts said nothing. Maher went on, 'So I was called to the scene of all this butchery in the middle of the night, and it ruined my beauty sleep, *compris*, chum? And it was ugly, and I've got two stiffs on my hands or so I thought at first, and I'm not very pleased about it. I've got nothing to go on and that's ruining my breakfast too. So eventually I track down Jenner here, with whom I have had dealings in the past, and of whom if I know nothing I know he is not in the business of shooty-shooty bang-bangs with French detectives, and he tells me all about being picked up by you in Paris and he tells me who the man with the holey bonce is and he even tells me that he's pretty certain the girl is a French detective. And I think to myself, "What a piss-off, Eamon. How unfortunate for this poor French girl detective! When I get hold of the paperwork and find out which English detective is supposed to be looking out for her I'm going to have his guts for garters; I mean, he's going to be a school crossing patrol from now on because he's a pillock." That's what I thought. So then I look for the paperwork on it. And I've got men turning NSY inside out and upside down, going through telexes and I don't know what. What did you say the French for "fucking prat" was, Jenner?'

'"Pillock" you asked. I don't know either of them.'

'Well, Mr Letellier, I'm beginning to think we've got one here, whatever the French for it is, and I mean it's not him and it's not me and it's not him. But we've got one here. Got it?'

Letellier said nothing.

'So eventually when we've gone through about a million pieces of paper and can't find anyone responsible for this French girl sleuth who is dead in Wapping, I'm forced to go humbly to this private detective creep here and ask "Who do you think could have sent her?" and he says "Ring Letellier". Letellier the prat . . . or is there some even bigger prat responsible for sending this girl here?'

'I sent her.'

'You sent her.' Maher paused, as if expecting Letellier to speak, then went on. 'Good. Jenner also tells me that he had gone to Paris in search of one Eleanor Wallace, who has done a bunk from her father, the aforementioned Charles Wallace with the holey head. And he says that she was the girlfriend of the dead half-English half-Italian you found in Paris, one Paolo Bianchi. And this Paolo Bianchi is the son of another Paolo Bianchi, and I think even *you* lot must know who *he* is. But throughout all that, throughout all these things happening, and dead men in Paris and you releasing English murder suspects to wander around England like an unexploded bomb with inept baby-girl detectives following, not one time, not once do you say to yourself . . . "I wonder what the telephone number of Scotland Yard is? I wonder if they'd have any opinion of all this? You never know, they might want to help me." This or a thought like it, it never crossed your mind.'

Letellier stood, stretched, then looked through the venetian blind. He pulled the slats apart with his fingers and pushed his eyes up to his fingers. I was standing next to him, and his face was close to mine, but I could see no sign of emotion on his face now.

'There are procedures, Mr Letellier. They're quite clear. Why didn't you use them? Don't you trust us?'

Letellier turned. 'There wasn't time.'

Roberts stood. His chair scraped. 'I have an appointment.' He banged the door after himself.

'He's not happy,' Maher said. 'Some of my colleagues want to drop you in it. Some of my colleagues think the best way to deal with you is to have the British Foreign Office call in your Ambassador and tell him what we think of DIY policing by foreign powers in England. And I reckon your Ambassador and your Ministry of Police would get a bit cheesed off with you, Mr

157

Letellier, for making them look stupid before all the world . . . for making them look illegal. Some of my colleagues want to make you a French school crossing patrol . . . or what do they do with failed detectives there? Make traffic wardens of them?'

'It was just time.'

'It was just *trust*. We're not that stupid here. You didn't tell us because you thought that instead of helping you, one of our chaps might have tipped off Jenner here he was being followed. But no one needed to tip him off. She was obvious. Jenner knew all the time he was being followed. I presume the person who shot your girl detective must have found her pretty obvious, too.'

We three were in silence for some minutes. I thought of the dead girl, half her face full of bullet holes. Her ghastly white flesh on the slab had made her look even younger somehow, and the image of Eleanor's face and Eleanor's skin came before me again and again.

'What will you do now?' said Letellier.

'Not what you think. I said some of my colleagues objected to your methods, and that some of them wanted to give you a political roasting. Not me, though, Letellier. If your government gets hounded about this it won't be because of the Metropolitan Police. It won't be because of me. I'm going to give you a break. You go back to France, be a good fellow, stop playing spies and stop blundering around England. *You* solve the murder of the Italian Englishman in Paris, *I'll* solve the murder of the French lady detective in England.'

'But they're the same case. They're connected.'

'Maybe they are. I don't know. If they are we'll go in for a bit of old fashioned co-operation. You phone me, I'll phone you. We'll swap information. I may ask you to come to England to help me again, I may ask to come to France and you'll have to tell me what to do there . . . tell me what the local rules are. We'll co-operate – a bit like the *Entente Cordiale*.'

'That led to the First World War,' I said. Maher didn't even acknowledge my existence.

'So there will be no question of dropping you in it, no question of telexes leaving New Scotland Yard saying "We demand, sack Letellier", as far as I'm concerned as long as our plan of action is clear. You go back to France and co-operate with me. I'll stay here and co-operate with you. We'll both get our jobs done. Savvy?'

Letellier nodded. 'I understand.'

Maher stood.

'So thank you for your identification and goodbye.'

Maher raised his hand. Letellier thought it was a friendly gesture, and half held out his before he realised Maher was indicating the door.

'Goodbye,' said Maher again. 'There'll be a car outside to take you back to Heathrow.'

'Don't you want my information on this case?'

Maher shook his head. 'We're already in contact with your colleagues through official channels. We already know as much as you do. Goodbye.'

Letellier left.

Maher smiled and shook his head. He gathered his papers. 'Come on, Jimmy. I'll buy you a drink and you give me the whole story.'

'In a pub?'

Maher waved at the room. 'I get sick of these places. I get sick of seeing mutilated and battered people.'

'I think Letellier is sick of it too. Do you know who killed this boy in Paris?'

'Letellier's colleagues think they do.'

'Do you know who killed this French policewoman?'

'I've got a description. I don't know who it is yet.'

'Firm description?'

'A man who was there in the area and no one can account for him. Dark-haired, thick-set, forties. Well dressed in a quiet sort of way.'

We were in a corridor now. I stopped. 'You didn't need Letellier at all, did you? You just got him over here so you could give him a good earwigging.'

Maher shrugged. A nurse came through swing doors at the far end of the corridor.

'You brought him here so you could humiliate him, isn't that right?'

'He humiliated himself. Now he has to go home and explain why the girl's dead. That's his problem. That's his responsibility. I'll do the detective work. That's mine. It's all been arranged with his bosses. It's my case now. They don't want it.'

'I'm not going to any pub with you.'

'You're shouting, Jimmy.'

'I'm off.'

159

'The pub or the nick. It's up to you, Jimmy. You'll come and hear me out.'

A uniformed policeman had followed the nurse through the swing doors. He was waiting for us.

'Sign off, Dusty,' said Maher, 'Mr Jenner and me, we're going for a drink.'

Chapter Thirty-one

Maher was in a peculiar mood even by his standards. He took me to a quiet pub just off the Hackney Road and treated me to a detailed résumé of Roberts's career. Maher didn't want to hear my story, he wasn't interested in Charlie Wallace's daughter, he didn't want to know about my trip to Paris. What Maher wanted was to tell me about Roberts. Then he left. Just like that.

*

By eleven I was in a foul-smelling phone box in Shoreditch, talking to Denis O'Keefe.

'I want Bianchi's address.'

'So what are you ringing me for?'

'Come on, Denis, you can get it.'

'How? It's eleven at night. After. Anyone I do know who has access to all that is going to be tucked up in bed with his cocoa and good book.'

'Try, Denis. Remember all the things I've done for you. Try.'

'Give us your number. I'll ring you back.'

Five minutes later he did.

'Bonar Street, number eleven. Very rich, very fancy address, Jimmy. As suits a bleeding criminal... makes you ill, doesn't it? What am I going to get out of all this? I presume you are chasing round after the addresses of retired Italian drug dealers in the course of some profitable employ?'

'Sort of. Are you saying you want some money from me, Denis?'

'Well, *something*. Let's say you owe me something. I'll let you know what. I'd better ring off now, or my wife'll think I've got a bint on the phone.'

'I have got something for you, Denis. I couldn't do it myself because I was too busy... but it's outside your line of work. You'll have to do it on the side, if you're to do it at all.'

'I'm listening.'

There was a couple waiting outside the phone box, and they'd been very patient. The man tapped on the window, apologetically.

'Only a few seconds more,' I said.

'What?'

'You'll have to do it on the side because it'll never look to your bosses as if you're investigating insurance work.'

'Don't you worry about them. I'll cope with them. What's the deal?'

'An eccentric millionaire, geezer from Northampton. Called Ronald Lasker. Aged around forty, medium everything according to his wife. Has these mental aberrations, probably guilt brought on by having all that dough. He runs away from home, makes out to be a down-and-out, tells people he's looking for work. Does it regularly. I mean it's very difficult for his family. If they put around just how barmy he was it would probably ruin his companies.'

The couple outside the telephone box had obviously got fed up waiting, and they started doing outside the box what they were going home to do anyway.

'So they want him found?'

'That's it. Find him and we'll go from there.'

'And how much have you quoted them?'

'Denis, where are your standards? These people are millionaires, you know? You'll be paid well. More than well. I've got to go now. Stay in touch.'

The Shoreditch street air was hardly less sweaty than the phone box. The waiting couple were almost incandescent, and ignored the empty phone box. I walked up to Dalston. It only takes fifteen minutes. Then I drove the Rover home and took my bomb upstairs. I put on some kitchen gloves and cleaned everywhere on the bomb Leon or Rainer or I could have touched. Then I put some double-sided tape on the casing. Then I took my clothes off and showered. By half-past midnight I was dressed again in sweatshirt, jeans and a cool mohair jacket,

162

bum-freezer style, which my ex-wife bought me on one of her 'smarten-up-Jenner' campaigns. I could have passed for an Italian myself, though disguise is not what I had in mind. I put a pair of driving gloves on, dropped the bomb and a large screwdriver in a carrier bag and went downstairs to the Rover. Half an hour later I'm outside the garage entrance to number eleven Bonar Street, Chelsea. The night is muggy and Jenner's sweating because he's scared of getting caught. There's more than a little elegance about attaching a bomber's bomb to his own car, though, and I was willing to suppress the fear as best I could and simply get on with it. The garage door was well locked with an Ingersoll padlock and hasp. The postern, though, had a silly little nightlatch. The bomb was in my mohair jacket pocket. One push on the door and I was in. Then I gently closed the door behind me, thumb over the knob. And for a moment I was completely alone in complete darkness. Or so I believed.

Chapter Thirty-two

I nearly came round a couple of times in the Mercedes. I had that half-feeling of consciousness. I was aware of traffic lights and of an awful pain in my head. I was aware of hands holding my head. They weren't my hands. I was aware of the Italian newspaper on the floor of the car. Di Nemico lay in the street. Then there was nothing. Then the car swerved and there was the sweet feeling of a woman by my side and it was her hands that were holding my head. Then there was nothing again. The journey in the Mercedes could have lasted an hour or a day or two minutes. I wouldn't have known.

*

There was a neon light right above me, and I was in a room alone. The room was quiet and clean and smelled fresh. I tried to sit up and someone drove a nail into my head. I moaned and fell back, then tried again. The door opened and Leila Lucas came in. A nurse followed. I was sitting on the edge of the bed. The nurse said, 'Now we must rest. Lie down.'

I'm afraid I swore at her.

'That won't do. That won't do at all.' The nurse put her hand on my chest. I pushed her aside. I was probably a little rough.

'I'll fetch the doctor,' she said and left the room in a swirl of starch and stiff-necked loftiness.

'I told them I found you on my doorstep, Jimmy, and that you'd had some sort of accident or been mugged or something and wandered to my flat.'

'Where are we now?'

'St Stephen's. They thought you would have concussion.'

'What's the time?'

'Ten.'

'So I've been out all night?'

'Yes.'

'I've got to get on, Leila.'

'Of course. But she's right. You'll have to rest, first.'

'Do you know what happened to me?'

'Yes.'

The nurse came in with a doctor, a slim Asian man with long, slender fingers and a sad expression. He told me I would be stupid to leave, but that the place wasn't a prison. I could go if I wanted. The nurse brought my bloody clothes.

'You look like a Sikh,' said the doctor and smiled. He pronounced it in the Indian way, 'sick'.

'Thank you. Do I have to keep wearing the turban?'

'No. The nurse will change it for you and give you a normal dressing. Do you remember what happened?'

'No. Nothing. Have you reported me to the police?'

'Reported what? When you remember, you report it. You have seventeen stitches in your scalp. My advice is stay here.'

'Seventeen . . . but no fracture?'

The doctor grinned. 'No fracture. Lucky. You have to sign these.'

*

On the Fulham Road Leila's BMW had a ticket but no clamp.

'How about your job?' I said.

'Gave it up. Actually it gave me up, if you want to know.'

'So what are you doing now?'

'Driving you to a clothes shop.' She giggled. A draught of air blew her bob of hair across her face for a second and she shook her head. 'And a hat shop. You'd look bloody funny walking around like that, Jenner.' I pulled down the sun-visor to look in the vanity mirror. My head was shaved on top and a big strip of pink adhesive plaster ran along the ridge that my stitches made. Leila accelerated the Beemer and I flipped the sun-blind up again.

'How did you end up looking after me, Leila?'

'Maggiera had you sent round to me.'

'Maggiera who?'

'Ricardo Maggiera. An associate of Paolo Bianchi's. He had some people bring you round to my flat last night. They asked if I could help you, seeing as I knew you.'

'Help him, more like.'

'Exactly. Maggiera turned up with a couple of heavies to protect Paolo when his son was killed. They were the heavies down by the gate of George Tiler's house when you came to George's party. You must have seen them.'

'In Wiltshire?'

'Where else? This should do.'

We were in Knightsbridge, outside a shop with a stark-looking window and no prices on the clothes.

'I can't afford to buy clothes here.'

'I can.' And she marched in. Double yellow line. Taxis bibbing their horns. People stared at me. I went in too.

*

I have no doubt that Leila Lucas is honest, but . . . but, but, but. According to her, these two 'protectors' of Bianchi's saw me going into his garage, bushwacked me and – convinced I was some sort of assassin sent to kill Bianchi – were just in the process of dealing with the problem on a permanent basis when Maggiera came into the garage to check out the fracas, found and recognised me and said something like 'No, don't chuck him in the Thames, boys, take him to hospital; Leila will help you.' So they did, being overcome with kindness all of a sudden. If they'd only looked under the wing of the Merc, they might have been less kindly disposed.

'Why did they bring me to you?'

'Well, it would look a little odd if you were brought into the hospital by these heavies, Jimmy.'

'You're mixing with a rough crowd. What did Maggiera say to you?'

'Nothing. He *sent* you, he didn't bring you. Paolo told him to have you sent to me.'

'Rough rough crowd. What's a nice girl like you doing hanging round with a mob like that?'

'I'm not. Bianchi has decided he's had enough of me. The visit to George Tiler's was a swansong. He went through with it just because he'd already arranged it. He's like that.'

166

'Dependable.'

'In a way. I don't care... there are plenty more men. What's a nice boy like you doing trying to break into his house?'

'I was looking for Eleanor.'

'Absolutely sparkling, sir. You really have got the figure for that jacket.' The salesman was wearing an outfit of stonewashed denim, he had a ring in his ear, very short hair and a bushy moustache. 'Would you like to try the trousers? They're 33, which is a little on the long side for sir. I wonder if you know your inside leg measurement?'

'Which one?'

He went off in search of his tape-measure and the trousers.

'I thought she might be hiding in Bianchi's house.'

'So why didn't you ring on the doorbell?'

'*Hiding*.'

'Well she's not. I'm certain.' Leila kissed me on the cheek. 'And he's right, you *have* got the figure for the jacket.'

Stonewashed denim came back bearing a tape-measure and a big smile.

'We can take them up right now if need be.'

I picked up the trousers. 'They'll do as they are.'

＊

We were back by Leila's Beemer. I was wearing a suit four sizes too big for me (which is thought trendy) plus a hat that would look overstated on Al Capone. What I needed was a pair of spats.

'So Mr Maggiera comes in, stops his hoods killing me, is told by Bianchi to send the upright cadaver round to your house and have you sort the situation out, which you agreed to do. What's more you sat by the invalid's bed all night like some romantic heroine. Am I being told I am a lucky fellow or what?'

'What. Don't take the hat off, it suits you.'

I'd already done it, though. You can't sit in a modern car in an Al Capone hat. We got in.

'Why did Bianchi leave you?'

'Oh stop asking questions.'

She rubbed her face with her hands. I could have sworn for a moment Leila was crying. Only for a moment.

'Why?'

'He didn't. I left him. He found out I was cheating on him. He

167

hit me, the bastard. Nowhere it shows, you understand, Jimmy. I don't know.' Leila shook her head violently. 'They're backwoodsmen, really. It's all blood, sweat, property and semen. It's all to do with dominate or be dominated. Honour and shame. The unfaithful wife.'

'You weren't his wife though.'

'It doesn't matter. He behaves as if he owns everyone and everything.'

'Does he own people? Does he own policemen?'

She sniffed. 'I don't think so. Paolo Bianchi is retired from his former "business", as he calls it. I've never known him to have any contact with a policeman. Not even when his son died.'

We were silent for a while.

'That's rough,' I said. 'Even for an old man it's rough to beat up women.'

'It's rough okay. I bloody hate him, Jimmy.'

She leaned on my shoulder and began soaking the shoulder-pad of my new suit.

'So why did you help cover for his hoods last night?'

Back down to a snivel. Noisy nose-blowing on tissue. Not like Leila.

'I don't know, Jimmy. For your sake, I suppose.'

I laughed. The sound rattled around my skull like a pebble. Leila looked sad and sober, suddenly. 'No one's ever hit me before and I swore no one ever would.'

'You helped last night because you're scared of him. Now you're buying me an expensive suit because you feel guilty. How did you ever get into this mess, a girl with your background? You should have gone to the police and charged him with assault. Now he's got you. You're scared and you'll do what he wants.'

'I'm scared and he is, Jimmy. That's his problem. He's lived here quiet and rich for a long time. Nobody's bothered him. Then there's this business with his son and he's dead scared. So am I, so are you. Look at you.'

Leila brushed my face with the back of her hand.

'Go away,' I said. 'Go and stay somewhere else until it all goes quiet.'

'It's gone quiet. Also I didn't buy the suit. Maggiera did. He thought what had happened to you was truly dreadful, and he gave me money to buy you some more clothes and some more cash for you.'

She lifted her handbag and pulled out a bundle of notes. 'What's Maggiera in all this?'

'Used to be a close associate of Paolo's in what they call "the old days". Paolo got very scared suddenly, some time before his son died. He never said what of, but I'm pretty certain he was frightened of some sort of violence. Then, when his son died, the violence had happened. Maggiera came over to provide Paolo's protection.'

'Where from?'

'Nice. He lives in Nice. He brought a couple of men with him and the plan was that the men should live in with Paolo. They were the men who clubbed you. Until last night, as far as I knew Maggiera was back home in Nice.'

'Frenchmen?'

'Italians. Maggiera is an American-Italian, like Paolo. But quite a bit younger.'

'How did Paolo react to his son's death?'

'Pretty sanguine, if you want to know. They'd had some sort of row. Paolo never forgave him and seemed more concerned with his own safety than anything else when he was told what had happened.'

I pushed the notes back into her handbag.

'Start the car, Leila. I want to go and pick up mine.'

She started the car and pulled into the traffic.

'Give Maggiera his money back and say "thank you but no thanks" from Jimmy Jenner.'

'I've no idea where to find him. I've only met him twice.'

'Describe him,' I said.

Chapter Thirty-three

Defoe Mansions looks gloomy even in the summertime. I plodded up the stairs with a head that was getting more and more sore. I was coffee-less, breakfast-less, dressed like an albino pimp and wondering how the hell I was going to find Letellier in the entire French police system, given my grasp of French. *Où est Letellier? Moi je suis détective Anglais. Non, pas de Scotland Yard.* They'd simply tell me to chuff off.

'I never thought to see you so *wonderfully* dressed, Jenner!'

Letellier was sitting at my kitchen table drinking coffee that smelled divine and smoking cigarettes that smelled slightly less divine.

'You can buy croissants in England. Isn't it *wonderful?* When I saw you parking I dropped one in the oven.'

'Popped, not dropped.'

He grinned. I said, 'Why are you here?'

'I have been suspended. Isn't it wonderful?'

'You'll wear that word out. It's not quite wonderful, anyway. Unless of course you've connived at being suspended. How's Meyer?'

'Wonderful. Have some coffee.'

I had some coffee, feeling like one of the three bears.

'Have you actually been out of England?'

'I think it's the hat that's the best part. I like the hat. I think you'll have to get some sunglasses, though. You're developing bruised eyes.'

'What did you do?'

'I went through Immigration, had a meal, couple of coffees,

170

then I went down one of those huge boarding corridors, turned right and became a passenger landing at Heathrow. I slept on your sofa. You should get better locks on your house.'

'If you get better locks they break the doorframe. It's better to rely on the door Entryphone for the extra bit of security you so easily overcame. Why are you here?'

'Jenner . . . why do you think? I want to find the man who killed my colleague, the girl for whom, as your Maher so elegantly pointed out last night, for whom I am responsible. The girl whose death he doesn't appear to be very bothered about investigating.'

'I'm not sure he isn't. You're here.'

'What does that mean, exactly?'

'They didn't accompany you out to the plane. Maher's a very thorough man. If he'd wanted to make sure you got on the plane, he'd have told his fellows to see you right to your seat and do up your lapbelt. Like you took me to Gare du Nord.'

'You think Maher *expected* me to come back?'

I sat very gently on the old leather sofa, nursing my coffee and my sore head.

'Yes, I think that's a very plausible construction. Last night was out of character for him, and he confused me for a while. Eamon Maher is the stiletto, not the bludgeon.'

Letellier lit another Gitane, puffing angrily. I went on.

'One way of seeing what he did to you last night is to think that he's simply a rude sod, pig-headed, nasty with it. He dragged you all the way from France not to identify the girl but so that you could be identified as the culprit in this game of not following procedures. He brought you here so he could humiliate you. That would be one way of looking at it. But there are two more ways of seeing it. One is that Maher is not a man given to making gratuitous insults, nor to wasting his own time. Why would he want to give you a telling off that your own bosses would presumably give you in France? And if you asked me is Maher the sort of man likely to bring you here, insult you and then tell you to bugger off I'd have to say, no. No, he wouldn't do that for mere dramatic effect. He *might* do it, though, for some practical effect. He might have done it thinking that by insulting you and telling you to bugger off you'd do exactly the opposite. And he might have thought that if he told you to lay off the murder of Marie Renan you might do the very opposite and give it a very close scrutiny.'

'Why would he do that?'

'Because *he* can't. Because Maher somehow thinks you'll carry out an investigation he can't.'

Letellier pulled at his lips as if they were putty to be moulded into the next expression. The next expression was sour.

'He can't make a good investigation, you're telling me. He can't give the business close scrutiny?'

Letellier said 'scrutiny' as if it had no vowels at all.

'That's one way of seeing it.'

'And you? Both you and his colleague, Roberts, were there. What does this "obtuse", as you call him, policeman want from you and from Roberts?'

'Me . . . nothing. Probably expects me to be your minder or something. Knows that'll keep me happy and I'll get a fee out of it for finding the girl. Roberts . . . well, I don't think, in this theory, he wants anything from Roberts at all. I think he was demonstrating to Roberts, showing that he could warn us both off. And if that was true it could only mean that Roberts is hiding something and that it's being connived at by his chums in New Scotland Yard. Some bigger fish they're going for, perhaps. It wouldn't be the first time they'd lied and cheated to get a man covered from one charge so they can get him and/or some bigger fish on another charge. And Maher has had to go along with it, which puzzles me, Letellier, because to my knowledge Maher is as straight as a die . . . definitely wouldn't do anything against the interests of justice as those interests are seen by Eamon Maher. In one evening I have seen him both being bloody rude to someone *and* behaving like the bent detective we all know and love from the movie screen. Either Maher is going through the menopause or he's up to something, and the something involves Bianchi, *père et fils*, you, your dead copper and Eleanor Wallace. Now you tell me.'

'Who is Roberts?'

'Detective Superintendent. Big wheel in charge of a tiny unit called DRIL, Drugs Information Liaison. Not that he should mean anything to you or anyone else. Maher was definitely hinting to me that he was giving you an earwigging – a telling off – for Roberts's benefit.'

'Why would he do that?'

'I don't know. Because of internal politics, because Roberts used to be on the Drugs Squad in the seventies with Maher and maybe he has something over him.'

'But why would Roberts want him to tell me off for show?'

I stood. Why does a pain in the head make the rest of you ache?

'You're the detective, Letellier. You tell me. Can you get through all doors like you did mine?'

'Of course not *all*. Give me your cup.' He went into the kitchen and fussed around with the washing-up. Maher's men had been careful and had tidied up after themselves. All my domestic servants are policemen. Letellier tapped the oven. 'Eat your croissant.'

'Maybe Roberts has something over Maher that's contrived, like your man in rue Bleue had over Eleanor. Or maybe something else. As I said, there are *three* ways of seeing it.'

Letellier put the cup and the tea-towel down. Slatted light shone through the window, drew dark bands on his hands. He rested his hands on the drainer.

'What does she say about the rue Bleue?'

'Nothing, except that she was arrested on a drugs bust coming from Italy with her boyfriend and that they were taken to Paris and that *she* alone was taken to meet a detective in the rue Bleue. Were you that detective, Letellier?'

'No. What did she tell you?'

'Not much. We were interrupted by her having an urgent need to go out. She said she was going out for cigarettes, but it's pretty obvious she went to meet her father and your colleague, Renan. My guess is that the meeting was arranged for Wapping and that when Eleanor Wallace got there she found her father and your colleague shot up and looking like dead. She came back here afterwards, but she wouldn't speak. Now she's gone. Your colleague in the rue Bleue put the frighteners on her, and she has been running ever since. And if you want to know, Letellier, I think it could be that *you* were the man in the rue Bleue. You were the one who put the scares into her, you were the one who manipulated her. Maybe you saw yourself as having the drop on Bianchi's son, and maybe you thought that would give you leverage on the man himself. Eleanor Wallace would be your "agent" – you specialise in putting women into danger, don't you? Only it all went wrong and the younger Paolo Bianchi ended up dead and Eleanor ended up running. So instead of playing out some master endgame you've got nothing . . . nothing except a dead boy, a dead detective, a girl on the run from both you and the Mafia.'

I walked back into the living-room. It's very queer to wear a hat indoors. I threw the hat on the sofa.

'And I've got a head full of stitches and a load of Italian bastards trying to kill me. All of that fits. All of that works. You're the man in rue Bleue. You're the one who's been manipulating this, and somehow Eamon Maher has got wind of it and decided to bring you here and show his former colleagues in the Drug Squad what low-quality bullshitters their great friends and allies across the English Channel are. How about that? Maybe Roberts has nothing on Maher. Maybe it's the other way round. Maher wants you to stay here and dig a big hole for yourself. Then he'll let you jump in it. That's the third way of seeing it, that he's dealing with a load of too-bleeding-clever-dick French cops, and he's going to give them – he's going to give *you* – every chance to make a fool of yourself over some ever so smart little piece of Euro-politics you've got going.'

'You don't believe that.'

'Why not?'

He came into the living-room too and lit another cigarette.

'Renan's last report was that she had discovered something very exciting and was leaving you alone for a few hours.'

'Go on. *What* was more interesting than me?'

He smiled wryly. 'She never said. It was a one-way message left on a telephone answering machine. Next thing, she was dead.'

'Rubbish. *What* did she see?'

'I really don't know. I'm not playing games here.'

'Of course.'

'Do you have a Fax machine?'

I mean, my furniture is only ever going to be firewood and scrap metal when I get finished with it. I have a manual typewriter, a collection of old biros, knackered-out filing cabinets, a couple of Kelly's Directories (out of date). A beaten-up sofa and a bottle of whisky. I poured a glass of whisky and didn't even bother answering him.

'If you have access to a Fax machine I can prove I wasn't the man in the rue Bleue. We only knew about the rue Bleue after we picked her up.'

'Ring Maher. He's probably got one. His address is in my book on the table.'

This time Letellier didn't bother answering.

Chapter Thirty-four

I lay on my back in Hyde Park. I wore sunglasses and my expensive suit. The hat rested part on the grass, part on my head. It was a warm day and a tractor-drawn mower rattled in the distance. The grass I lay on had been recently cut by the same mower and the smell filled my nostrils. Children ran past, giggling. An Arab woman wearing a hundred yards of black net curtains chased the children, neither laughing too nor calling the children back to her. There was only the sound of her shoes scuff-scuffing on the ground as she ran past. Then a shadow cast over me and Letellier said, 'I've got them.'

He sat cross-legged by my side and slapped the papers he held on my chest.

'How well can you read French?'

'You know I can't.'

He began to read slowly in English, translating from the papers.

'I do certify that this is a true record of the interrogation of Eleanor Jane Wallace by sub-commissioner August Meyer, interrogation carried out before me and witnessed by me . . . and then that's signed by me. Look, you can see.' He held the papers out for me to see.

'Carry on.'

'Okay. Then there's a lot of stuff about where she lives and who she is and all that. You're not interested in that.' He flipped over two pages. 'Here. This is the part. Meyer says, "Tell me again about the man in rue Bleue."'

'Eleanor Wallace says, "Tell you what? His false name?"'

' "Describe him." '

' "The man in the rue Bleue was called Monsieur Leonard. He was middle-aged. Mid-forties. Very dark hair, very dark complexion, as if he would be a Corsican or something like that." '

' "Was he French?" '

' "Of course. He worked for the French Secret Service. He told me. He made no attempt to convince me that Monsieur Leonard was his real name. He let me understand he had a close relationship with the anti-terrorist police." '

' "Did he show you any form of identity?" '

' "No. What if he had? It would have been fake. The main thing was that Leonard had me in his grip and I couldn't get out except by co-operating with him." '

' "Do you know where he lived? Did he talk about colleagues, friends, associates? Sources of information, even?" '

' "No." '

' "So what was he like?" '

' "I told you. Dark. Southern. Middle-aged. Running to fat. He didn't bother shaving a lot. He told me that I knew the leading members of a radical group, what he called a 'group of left-wing terrorists'. He said Tom Smith was the moving force and that I was going to penetrate them. I was going to become his – that is M. Leonard's – informer, bought and paid for. Simple." '

' "Or what?" '

' "Or we, that is Paolo and me, we would rot in jail for twenty years. They would ensure it. I was to become intimate with Tom Smith again, I was to become a member of his group. I was to pass back to Leonard what I learned." '

' "How were you to achieve this?" '

' "By becoming intimate with Tom Smith." '

' "Physically? By intimate you mean 'sleep with'?" '

' "Yes." '

' "And did you?" '

' "Yes." '

' "Did you stay with Smith all the time from when you were picked up by these 'police' on the way from Italy until the Di Nemico incident?" '

' "Yes. Except for twenty-four hours in London. My father was having a book published and needed me to be there. He's a drunk. I went there and arranged for a private detective to look after him, which is all he needed. Looking after.''

'"And during all this time you kept in touch with M. Leonard how?"

'"Most of the time by phone. A couple of times I went to the office in rue Bleue.''

'"Did you keep a note of the phone numbers?"

'She did.' Letellier broke off from his reading for a moment. 'All call boxes, of course. Next, Meyer asked her, "What did you do all the time?"

'"I was with Tom and the others.''

'"What did they do?"

'"The same as ever. They lay around drinking. They talked tough. Every now and then they would go out in the middle of the night and paint a slogan on a wall. They were the most incompetent terrorists in the world. I reported it all to M. Leonard. I told him he was wasting his time.''

'"In person?"

'"No. By phone.''

'"What did he say?"

'"That he would decide. That I should do what I was told and everything would go fine for Paolo and me.''

'"Where was your young boyfriend during all this?"

'"Locked up in Saint-Denis with one of a team of detectives who were taking it in turns to stay with him.''

'"And this was an open-ended arrangement? You did not know how long you would be Tom Smith's unwilling 'concubine' for?"

'"Three months. Leonard said that if I did it for three months they would let us both go and destroy the evidence. I just had to keep them informed for three months and that would be it. We would be free.''

'"Did the man Paolo Bianchi know what you were doing?"

'"He knew the deal. He knew I was being asked to become an active member of Tom Smith's group and give information on them.''

'"But not about the physical intimacy?"

'"We never discussed it.''

'"And you did this for three months?"

'"Less. Leonard set up a plan to catch them. A coup. He made it clear it would be a coup because, excuse me, but because

177

the French police, he said, aren't very good at catching people like Tom. He said people very high up in the government were keen to catch Tom and his group but that there must be no hint of illegality. No midnight confessions, no duress. They must be caught clean."

'"How many friends?"'

'"Four. All men."'

'"What about his girl associate, Claudine Leclerc?"'

'"I'm told she was distressed when you people released her. That she threw herself under a train. I never saw her again and Leonard assured me there was no chance of Tom Smith and his friends knowing she'd been in custody. The security was high, just like it had been with Paolo and me. That's what Leonard said."'

'Eleanor's very cool here,' I said. 'It sounds a lot cooler than the kid I know.'

'She was cool, Jenner. What can I tell you? That's how she was. Shall I go on?'

The tractor had pulled its mower away. The sound of the traffic in Knightsbridge seemed dulled for a moment. No kids were running around, no horses clip-clopping round the park. Suddenly Hyde Park seemed dead quiet. Flat calm.

'I don't believe it,' I said. 'I don't believe she was that cool.'

'This is an accurate history.' Letellier waved the papers. 'I brought them for you to see for yourself.'

'Not that. Something else.' I sat up. People seemed to move again, as if a film was starting up. Letellier began to read again.

'Meyer asked, "What was the plan M. Leonard put to you, Mademoiselle Wallace?"'

'"To kill Di Nemico."'

'"Who killed Di Nemico?"'

'"Tom Smith. Jean-Marie Chantin. Bruno Werner, Verner, some name like that. It's a false name. A man called Péguy, spelt like the poet, and myself."'

'"You killed Di Nemico?"'

'"I was there. I did as much as the man who pulled the trigger."'

'"Who pulled the trigger?"'

'"Tom and Bruno."'

'"Tom Smith and the man you knew as Bruno Werner or Verner? They pulled the trigger. They did the shooting?"'

'"Yes."'

'"Would you like a glass of water?"

'"No. I'm okay. Go on."

'And then, before Meyer could ask her another question she said, "It wasn't actually supposed to happen, of course. It went wrong."

'"Tell me the plan. Tell me from the beginning."

'"The plan was simple. The plan was that I should suggest Di Nemico as a target. They would agree. They would go to try to kill him. They would be caught by M. Leonard's people and the anti-terrorists. That would be the coup M. Leonard was seeking."

'"But what the plan itself was, what the strategies were, not just the effect Leonard wanted, do you understand?"

'"Okay. Di Nemico was thought of as a soft target. He was, as you know, an ex-minister in the Italian government. The 'ex' was important because, although there would be security it would be relatively weak and it would be provided by the French who would not believe Di Nemico was a man of any particular significance – as I could tell Tom. The real advantage of the protection being provided by the French was that they would be warned. The plan was to catch us. Me too, I was to be caught too. For effect. Leonard put it together for me and I was supposed to suggest this to Tom and Bruno. Di Nemico was supposed to visit the university, where he had been a lecturer in the 1960s. Then he would return to his accommodation, which would be in an apartment overlooking the river. Quai de la Tournelle. His security men should be relaxed by then, is how I put it to Tom, and the attack could be made outside the apartment block. Two should attack, two wait with motorcycles to escape. The escape would be across the Ile Saint-Louis. One of the bridges is permanently blocked off with chains, so there would be no question of a pursuit. In fact, Leonard said, Di Nemico would not be Di Nemico but a substitute in body armour. It would never come to a shoot-out. Tom and the others would simply be caught, snap!"

'"And this Leonard would allow you to go free, snap?"

'"That was the plan."

'"And how did you explain coming by the information about Di Nemico's trip?"

'"My godmother works in the university. I would say that I'd heard her discussing the details of the visit with a colleague, and that I'd built it all on that."

'Is this enough, Jimmy Jenner?'

'It's going to rain.'

Letellier stood. He held his hands out to feel the air.

'I don't believe so.'

'It's going to rain. Let's walk.' I stood too. We made our way down to the path that orbits Hyde Park. Horses trotted through dust near us. Their hooves sounded where the dust had worn out. Then there were trees, then the road. Big glossy cars flashed between the trees.

'Let's go right across to Green Park,' I said. We walked through the soft shade of the trees, then crossed the road, then went into the stinking tunnels under Hyde Park Corner. A boy played a guitar badly. Letellier gave him some money.

*

'She was tricked, wasn't she?'

'I thought so. Others weren't so sure. Meyer and I decided she had no criminal intent and we let her go.'

Now we were in Green Park. Tall dark trees and the high wall of Buckingham Palace. Above us was the madness of Piccadilly.

'Don't make me laugh. You know why you let her go as well as I do. You wanted to see what she would do, and who she would see.'

'We wanted to see what her boyfriend would do, if you want to know, Jenner.'

I sat on a bench and held my hand out for Letellier's official document. It's no good riffling through page after page you simply can't understand. I gave it back.

'How much more interview is there?'

'Lots more. It covers all sorts of things.'

'Does it cover the shooting of Di Nemico?'

He nodded and sorted through the pages, then began to read again.

'Meyer asked, "How did you get the guns there?"'

'"I carried them. I took them with some shopping in a bag, under a newspaper. There's the café by the apartment block. I sat there with the bag beside me. Right on time, Tom and Bruno turned up. Jean-Marie and Péguy were on the corner with their motorcycles. Di Nemico and two security men turned up. I spotted M. Leonard standing on the other side of the road – it's quite wide at that point. Leonard was alone with his back to the embankment wall, leaning against the stone. Watching. Tom and Bruno walked quickly to my table and took their guns from the shopping bag. They were little machine-guns. Neat-looking things. I put money on my table for my bill, then I stood. Tom and Bruno walked up to the security men and Di Nemico and began firing. There was blood everywhere. Tom and Bruno walked calmly away, but there were three dead men on the steps of the apartment block. No sign of Leonard's police, no sign of a special squad to snatch them. No sign of the body armour Di Nemico was supposed to be wearing. I was frozen to the spot. I've told you all this."

'"I know. Tell it again."

'"Traffic passed. The motorcycles had gone with the men on them. People seemed to wake from a dream. The waiter even came out and picked up the money I'd left on the table. Then a woman started screaming and it went on and on. A siren approached. Closer and closer. I walked away, along boulevard Saint-Germain. Then I took the Métro across to La Fayette to see if this M. Leonard hadn't arrived back there yet. Something had clearly gone badly wrong. His police hadn't been there, and all the other stuff that *wasn't* supposed to happen *had* happened."

'"What did you think had gone wrong?"

'She made no reply. Meyer asked her, "What did you do next?"

'"I was terribly confused. I didn't know what to do. When I arrived at the rue Bleue office things became worse instead of better. Leonard had disappeared. His office was deserted, then a security man from a clothing company on the floor below came up and asked what I was doing. I said I was looking for the occupant of this office. He said 'Are you on something? This place has been deserted for months.' He threw me out. I rang the flat in Saint-Denis about a thousand times, but there was no reply. I didn't dare go there. I stood outside a television dealer's near the Gare du Nord and watched the pictures of the shooting. Di Nemico and his guards, one Italian, one French, were dead. The police thought it was something to do with the Red Brigade in Italy, owing to Di Nemico having been a law-and-order man."

'"And then?"

'"And then I decided I should go home to my father. I nearly did, but I couldn't tell him what had happened, of course. And then I decided I must, even though I couldn't tell him. So I went to England straight away. Without going to Saint-Denis, without going to my flat – my own flat – which I was convinced would be crawling with police. I ate a hamburger and walked around the area of the Gare du Nord for a long time. I was there all evening. At one point I bought a cheap bag and some cheaper dresses. I'd thrown my shopping into a bin back in Saint-Germain because I thought it might have gun grease or something on it. Then I went into the station and bought a night train ticket to London."

'"Why did you buy dresses?"'

'"Because the border police and Customs would think it odd if I had no luggage at all."'

Letellier folded the A4 pages and put them inside his coat.

'That's as much as there is for you. Do you still believe I'm Monsieur Leonard?'

'I never did, seriously. I think I know who he is, though.'

'Who?'

'I think he's the same man who killed your colleague. I think I know where he was and who sheltered him when he did it. But there are other things that worry me about this, Letellier, not least the position of Eleanor Jane Wallace.'

'Because you can't find her?'

'Finding her is not the problem. Look, be a good fellow. I feel dreadful. Go and stand at the side of the road there and hold your arm out. Sooner or later a cab's going to stop. Tell him we're going to the Tower of London.'

'Why?'

'Because we're actually going to Wapping, but if you say "Take me to Wapping" you get a lot of sauce out of them because they're lazy bastards only fit for running Arab princes between whores' beds in Mayfair. And they don't want to go east. Now go and hold your arm out.'

Part Three
The Last Leg

Chapter Thirty-five

'Do you think you could break down doors, you know, with your shoulder? Like they do in films?'

I was leaning my walking-stick against an Entryphone button. Letellier was leaning his shoulder against an iron-reinforced warehouse door, as it had once been. Now it was an iron-reinforced door to stop the *hoi polloi* getting into the flats the warehouse had become. Letellier grinned and touched the door.

'Not this.'

'Who is it?' coughed the machine.

'Jenner.'

'I'm busy now, Jimmy. I've got clients with me. Come back in an hour.'

'No. I can't. I've got some papers that Frames-Pargeter left in my motor.'

'Well, put them into my mailbox.'

'No. They're too important for that. I have to give them to you in your hand. You'll be happier. So will Frames-Pargeter.'

There was a buzz and the door gave. I followed Letellier up the stone stairs.

*

George had an ageing pop star with him. The pop star had hair like Rod Stewart, a silk shirt like Mick Jagger and a wife like an Afghan hound. They were kneeling on the floor of George's flat/studio and they were admiring a model George had made so that the couple could bamboozle the planning authorities, spend millions and make millions more by turning their country pile into a country club. The woman leaned towards the model as if it was a new-born baby.

The ageing pop star ran his fingers through his knife-and-fork haircut and stood.

George said, 'What the hell happened to you?'

'I was clobbered. I want them to leave.'

'Where are the papers?'

'Don't worry about the papers, cock. Just get shot of these two berks. Then we'll talk.' I held my hat up. 'Look. I got clobbered right on my nut.'

The Afghan gave an aesthete's squeal. I said, 'Leave.'

George shook his head. 'Later. This is a very important meeting and I'm sure you know who my clients are.'

'Cabinet Minister, is he? Have I introduced my friend? He's Inspector Letellier, of the Sûreté in Paris. He's got the hump because one of his colleagues bought her ticket on the eternal bus right outside here. Now leave, you two.'

The pop star shook his head. I said to Letellier, 'Break something.'

Letellier stood on the model of the country club. The pop star looked at George for advice.

'Break something else,' I said. Letellier lifted a coffee table from the ground and hurled it against the wall. It smashed. The wall dented.

'I'm going to call the police,' the ageing pop star said.

'No police,' said George. 'No police. I'll call you later. Just go for now and I'll call you later.'

'Will you be all right with these two lunatics?'

Letellier picked up a large, Chinese-looking vase with a lamp set in the top. He pulled the plug from the mains and walked across to George's panoramic window over the Thames. He pushed the window open.

'I'll be fine. He's an old friend.' George pointed at me. The pop star shrugged and left with his Afghan, who wept a little and muttered to him in an extremely nasal accent.

'George, you have got into these people over your head, which was stupid. Now you're going to tell me exactly what happened.'

'I can't.'

Letellier dropped the lamp. Four floors. Splash. He closed the window. He turned to George.

'Do you swim?' Letellier said. George shook his head.

'Dirty down there. You next.'

Now all of George shook. I said, 'I'll tell you what I know, then you'll tell me.' I stood and tucked my walking-stick in my top pocket, then put my arm round George's shoulders. We walked through the debris of his model to where Letellier stood.

'*Wonderful* view,' Letellier said. 'I never knew there were such wonderful views in the East End of London.'

'George, you became indebted to these people. You did it to get Terence Gilligan off your back. He hadn't only approached you for money, there was Tony Frames-Pargeter too. Tony described him to me. He didn't know his name, but it was definitely Gilligan who'd approached him. You asked Bianchi if he or one of his pals could get Gilligan off your back. Am I right? *That* was your debt.'

George was really shaking. 'It wasn't Terence and it wasn't the money. It was that black ponce who lives with him putting him up to it.'

'Hadn't they gone to Italy?'

'Not by then. Now not at all. I asked an associate of Bianchi's, not Bianchi himself, if he knew someone who could scare the black boy off.'

'And did they?'

'Yes. No one has seen him since; so that's pretty thoroughly scared off, I should think.'

'Or dead. This person had him killed, didn't he, George?'

George began to shake even more, and his voice was thick with emotion. 'So I was told a couple of nights ago. But I swear I didn't ask them to kill him.'

'Just rough him up. Put the scares into him?'

He nodded. Letellier stared steadfastly through the window. Bermondsey glinted in afternoon sunlight below him.

'And then you owed this person one. Then you would be pals together when he asked you to pay the debt back. And he only wanted a small thing, he only wanted you to let him know what Eleanor Wallace was up to and when, and you only told him that she'd made an appointment to meet her father downstairs from here, another one of her "desperately needing and loving Daddy scenes", eh? And then you heard cars backfiring in the middle of the night and what do we know, Maggiera has done it again! Only this time personally, not through one of his button men. And Ricardo Maggiera comes up to your flat with the smoking gun and says, "George, George, you got to make it look like I'm one of your pick-ups, okay? You owe me this one, George. Remember Gilligan's boyfriend, George? Well he's filling the bellies of a thousand Dover soles by now and you're implicated, so for now just hide me in your bed and turn the boys in blue away." And so you did, George. So you did. Because you owed him one. That's why you couldn't have had Frames-Pargeter round here. That's why you asked me to head him off. I suppose Frames-Pargeter had already met him, yes? *He'd* have smelt a rat if he'd found Maggiera lain in your bed like some rent boy.'

I stopped. George didn't speak. Letellier said softly, 'Where's the gun?'

George opened the window again and pointed to the river. 'Down there. He threw it in the river when he came up.' He was silent again for a while. We two just stood by George's side and he stared at the river. Then he said, 'But you're not completely right. I never told Maggiera that Eleanor was staying here. I wouldn't have done that to her. I knew there was some feud over Bianchi's dead son and I would never have let it be known that Eleanor had this meeting here with her father. It was all a mistake, I discovered...'

'Of course it was a mistake. Being born is a mistake, George. Having him in here was a mistake. Knowing Eleanor was a mistake. Eleanor had arranged to meet her father outside here, maybe even *in* here, I don't know. The policewoman Renan had made contact with Charles Wallace and he brought her along. Maggiera turns up ready to shoot Eleanor and discovers instead that "she" appears to be sitting in a car with her father, just down from here. So he gives it to them both, bam! bam! Right in the head. Only it was dark and the car was unlit and he hadn't shot Eleanor. He'd shot Detective Renan, who is the former colleague of Letellier here, the chap with the long face. Now you know what he's unhappy about. Okay?'

'I didn't tell him. I don't know how he knew they were coming here but I wouldn't have told him.'

'Well *someone* did, and the girl detective got shot anyway. You figure it out.'

'I can prove I didn't. I know where Eleanor is now. She's hiding in Leila Lucas's flat. If I wanted to, I could've told Maggiera that . . . but I didn't.'

'Why is she there?'

'Because she thinks no one will look for her there. That's what she said.'

'And how long's she going to stay there? Till Maggiera and Bianchi die of old age?'

'Till she can get hold of you, Jimmy. That's what she said.'

I clapped my hands at Letellier. 'Come on, cocker. We're in a rush.'

I walked across the room, expecting him to follow. I heard a scuffle behind me. I opened the door. The scuffle had turned into a fight. I went back in time to see George's feet disappearing over the shallow sill of his panoramic window.

'He's fallen in the water,' said Letellier. I pointed to the phone.

'Nine-nine-nine. Ask for the river police. Ask or he'll drown.'

'It's not far to the waterside.' Then Letellier walked past me. I made the call myself, then went downstairs and told him off. Letellier didn't seem to hear me. Then I went and called Maher and challenged him. He didn't deny what I said. I didn't think he would.

*

We sat in Wapping tube station. About once a week there's a train up to Whitechapel. Marc Brunel's tunnel will last a million years.

'Of course we know of Maggiera. How could we not?'

'I have wondered.'

'But that he and Leonard were the same man, no. How can he be sure he won't meet Eleanor Wallace in London and be recognised? They are part of the same circle, after all.'

'I've had my doubts about that. I think the answer is that they're actually *not* part of the same circle, and I think he might have been certain of not meeting her because her contacts with Bianchi senior, like his, would be entirely predictable. And he was doing the predicting.'

'How?'

'At first through the son, I think. Now on his own account. I rang Eamon Maher and asked him if all that nonsense with Roberts the other night is because Bianchi senior is not a retired Mafia man nor a retired dope importer. I said, "Eamon, I think you weren't being entirely honest with me when you had your little shout and yell at Letellier there, and I'm not happy,

189

Eamon, because you could have got the two of us killed playing that particular game. That bastard Bianchi's active, isn't he?" And he said, "Roberts thinks so. But Roberts has got people on to it and these people are very exposed. Roberts doesn't want the pitch queered." And I said, "It comes to something when a murder investigation is queering a pitch, I mean where have you people left your values?" And he said, "It's not just the one murder, Jimmy, and it's not just the one pitch queered."'

'What?'

'He doesn't want anyone's big feet in his cabbage patch.'

Letellier laughed. 'That's no better!'

'Oh you know ... anyway, I told him he'd better get himself a warrant and look at Superintendent Roberts's bank accounts and stuff of that nature, because the only man queering pitches is Roberts and that makes a man feel a bit suspicious.'

The train came in carrying a load of dead-beats, some working women and one punk wearing headphones that were loud from the outside. Letellier brushed a seat with his hand, then sat. I just sat. Too tired.

I said, 'Bianchi's "activeness" makes a powerplay of the stuff in Paris. Maggiera and Bianchi's son wanted to make it difficult for Bianchi to stay in business, so they manipulated these crazy kids to kill Di Nemico. Everybody thinks ...'

'That Bianchi senior had Di Nemico killed. Nobody in France does, Jimmy, I can tell you. We didn't just *presume* it.'

'Yeah. But it makes the British police anxious. And it makes Bianchi's former associates definitely nervous. He can't go anywhere without everyone knowing what he's doing, who he's doing it with, and all that caper.'

'Why is the son Bianchi in on this? How do you know?'

'Because he'd have to be a particularly dumb bastard not to see through all this "Sit in a room for three months and let your girl do the work, baby". He was in this with Maggiera, I'm sure.'

Letellier nodded slowly. 'And then Maggiera had the boy killed?'

'I don't know about had him killed. I'm sure Tom Smith and his friends did it, because there would be no other reason to torture him, not for anyone else. Someone slipped to Smith and the boys that they'd been had, conned, and that the someone who'd had them was Eleanor's boyfriend. That's how I see it. They missed Eleanor but they certainly got the boyfriend.'

190

I suppose we both thought then of the pantomime in the French mortuary with Paolo's body. I know I did.

'So this means only one person can possibly tie Maggiera to M. Leonard and then to this "powerplay", as you call it. And she didn't know, maybe doesn't even know now that she has this information, Jimmy?'

'Maybe she does *now*. She was plenty scared enough when she came back to my flat after seeing what looked like her father's dead body. If she realises she was put up to this by her boyfriend and "Leonard", and if she realises that with the boyfriend dead and Bianchi wobbling there's only one person who can tie Maggiera into all this, and if he can get rid of her he's top of the pile and clean, too; I tell you chum, if that girl can do two plus two and figures that out, she'll be scared enough.'

'Why be so sophisticated? Why hasn't Maggiera simply had Bianchi the father shot by an assassin?'

'(a) Not easy. (b) Certain elements in his own organisation would think Maggiera is a man to make you watch your back when you're around him. This would not be to his advantage, I think. Maggiera is better having his work done at third hand and just happening to be the beneficiary. I'm sure he only came to kill Eleanor personally because there's no other way. Now he's blown it, he'll be a worried man, I should say. He can't go back to Nice and leave her wandering the streets and liable to go round to Paolo Bianchi's house any day and describe M. Leonard to the old boy. Maggiera has to stay here and tough it out. Tell me, how and why did you pick Eleanor up?'

'Information. A tip.'

'Who from?'

Letellier shook his head. 'I don't know. I think it was anonymous. Someone saying that he recognised an English girl sitting at the bar on the quai de la Tournelle when Di Nemico was shot.'

'He or a she?'

'I don't know. I can find out.'

We reached Whitechapel. The working women, Letellier and me got off. The dead-beats and the punks stayed on. Maybe the punk simply hadn't realised. Anyway he sat there.

Letellier said, 'I think we'd have found her anyway. There was a witness description of a girl at that café, from the waiter, and we were going through all the people who knew of the itinerary, plus all their contacts.'

'Yeah. You'd have found her by the turn of the century. Was she difficult to break?'

'No. Not really. She's not much more than a child, Jimmy.'

'And then when you'd done with her, you let her go to see what she would do next. And what she did next was phone me and say "Come see me in the Hotel Berry".'

He smiled but said nothing. The District Line train came in.

*

Leila's Beemer was there, but she didn't answer her door. Letellier let us in. Eleanor was sitting in the living-room. The room was an odd mixture of William Morris and Bauhaus, as if the only thing the furniture and fabrics had in common was that they'd once been in a magazine. But not on the same page. Eleanor had a gun levelled at us, a little pistol.

I sat too. 'That door's no good. Did you see how easily he came through there? Like a ghost, Eleanor. I tell you, going round this city with Letellier is a real education. You *do* know each other?'

She let the gun fall and nodded.

'It's not safe here,' I said. 'We'd better go.'

'Where?'

'Somewhere safe to have a chat. Then I'm afraid we have to go and talk to the boys in blue and give them the whole story.'

'Have you seen my father?'

'Through a window. I'm sure he'll be up and cursing, soon. Give me the gun.'

She gave me it. I waved Letellier towards the door.

'Go and have a look at the street, cocker. If you fancy it's all clear, hail a cab.'

'Where to this time?'

'The Imperial War Museum. We're going out to Brixton, but for God's sake don't tell them that. Just "Imperial War Museum" in your best French accent.'

Letellier went to check the street. After a few minutes there was a whistle and we went down too.

*

There was the sound of thunder.

'A train,' I said. We were in Leon's glass office at the back of his under-arch garage. There was instant coffee in cups before us. Greasemarks on the table. Leon had his boys working in the yard, so the workshop beyond the glass office was hidden in a darkness which was hardly penetrated by the neon lamps. The hoist stood like a medieval torture machine. The sunlit yard was a projection. The tall door to the yard was a cinema screen. The men outside were flickering ghosts. This greasy table and this greasy conversation was the real world.

'What you would have us believe, Eleanor, is unbelievable. Do you know that?'

'No. I don't know what I would have you believe.'

'I think you do. Have you ever been to the South of France?'

'Yes. Of course.'

'Recently?'

'Of course. It's not Scotland. People from Paris go all the time. I have friends there. What is this?'

'Last couple of months? Have you been in the last couple of months?'

She didn't answer.

'Let me tell you what I think you would have us believe, Eleanor. And if you find anything wrong with it, you just go right ahead and correct me.'

'Okay. If that's what you want.'

'You're very young, Eleanor, and I'm very suggestible. You turned up in London looking like a lost lamb, asking me to look after your father who was being an absolute A1 swine to you. Well, he was, there's no doubt about that. But you weren't all you seemed. Just a little while before that you'd been nicked by someone who claimed to be the French police for carrying a car load of coke – that much you admitted to. But then you say you were made – under duress – to help a mysterious French copper called "Leonard". Well, maybe you were the victim of a scam, but I'm pretty sure this "Leonard" is one and the same as a fruity-pie called Maggiera, and I think this man must have known your boyfriend. And then the next thing I'm asked to believe is that this Maggiera – Monsieur Leonard to you – puts you up to having a bunch of young lunatics kill Di Nemico. And you *did* it. You admitted as much to Letellier here . . . am I right?'

Eleanor nodded. Behind her Leon was yelling at a mechanic.

193

She was in artificial light, Leon was in sunshine. I could see Leon yelling but not hear what he was yelling. Letellier took his document out and spread it on the greasy table-top.

'Here's the record of what you said.'

'Okay.'

'It appeas that your boyfriend is after a big cut of his father's business here, and it appears that he has joined forces with Maggiera to make things look bad for Paolo senior. If Di Nemico is murdered everyone will presume Paolo senior had a hand in it; no more making out to be just an ex-Mafia man who has co-operated with the authorities and just happens to be the only *ex*-Mafia man in all eternity who they've never sent anyone after. No no. Di Nemico puts Bianchi the father out of business by *dying*, which idea I'm sure left Di Nemico's spirit happy if nothing else. This leaves Maggiera and your boyfriend in sole position to pick up the pieces. They're doing fine, Paolo senior is out. You still don't know anything about all this, you claim, so that when Maggiera decides to clean up completely by having your boyfriend killed this is also a complete surprise to you. The method used by Maggiera is of course brilliant. He gets your chums to do it. He tells them that they've been conned, and that Paolo is doing the conning and that he can be found in Saint-Denis. Tom Smith, Bruno and the rest of them, they get a bit cheesed off when they receive this information, and they go and take it out on Paolo. This is tough on Paolo, but it does leave Maggiera top of the said pile. I take it all this getting dressed up in yellow and all that caper is a big put-up to hide their trail, yes?'

'Yes. They've done it before.'

'Good. We're that far. And that's where I turned up in Paris and Paolo junior turned up dead.'

She nodded again. Leon was yelling and shooing his men around now, like an old mother hen. He came into the dark workshop and started burrowing in steel boxes behind the hoist.

'And you're unaware of any of this, Eleanor. Just a dupe. Hard luck on you.'

Again, 'Yes.' Coldly.

Leon reappeared holding two shotguns, like John Wayne on a good Saturday afternoon. There was a box of shells tucked under his arm. He came into the glass office.

'There's some blokes outside with shooters. They don't look like coppers to me.'

'It's illegal for people with a criminal record to hold firearms,' I said.

Leon pushed us through the door. 'Well aren't you bloody lucky I don't know that, Jim-boy? I've got a blue Ford Cortina outside the front. There's the keys. All you've got to do is get out there.'

A head peeked round the door from the yard. Leon fired from the hip. I pushed Eleanor behind the hoist. The head peeked again, this time accompanied by shots from a handgun. Then there was quiet, then a man ran across the sunlit yard. Letellier hit him with the other shotgun. The dark figure spun forward, a tumbling silhouette, then lay still. There were two more shots. Letellier and Leon fired back, their gunshots crashing like falling sheet metal against the bare brickwork of the workshop. The muzzles flashed brilliant yellow-white light in the darkness. The man by the door came round the corner firing, thinking the shotguns were unloaded. I squeezed the trigger on Eleanor's little revolver and he turned as if he'd been punched on the shoulder. He raised his gun again towards me. I pulled the trigger twice more. He sat down heavily, as a child might. Then his head fell backwards and cracked against the oily concrete of the workshop floor. A siren sounded in the distance. Two men came through the door this time, one fired his gun wildly, the other grabbed the man on the concrete floor and dragged him back.

'Don't shoot!' I called. 'Let them get out.'

They grabbed the one in the yard the same way, aimless pistol firing. Then there was the screech of tyres. Then there was quiet.

'Pick up the shell cases from your shotguns. Bring them.'

I pushed Eleanor out to the Ford. There was a pool of blood in the yard and a trail where the feet had dragged. Another train went over as I started the car. Letellier and Leon climbed in the back. Sunlight streamed through the windscreen. The street was empty.

'Push the guns to the floor,' I said. 'Under the front seats.' I drove slowly away. Two police cars passed us, going towards Leon's garage. Sirens and blue lights.

'Slowly, slowly,' said Letellier.

I stopped in Brixton Road. 'What you do, Leon, is buy yourself a Jamaica Pattie, stroll back to your garage and say "All right, John, what's supposed to be going on here then?" to the old bill.'

195

'What about me shooters?'

'Stick them under your arm and take them back now if you want.'

'Okay, okay. You was followed, Jim-boy. Someone's been staking this girl out. Someone wants her, ooh bad, like.'

'No, Leon. Someone wants me.' I got out too and stood beside him. 'You drive, Letellier. The manual murders my leg.'

Leon laughed.

'I'll make it up to you,' I said. 'I don't know how yet, but I will.'

He laughed again. 'Pay your bloody garage bill. Give me some money, I haven't got a bean on me.'

I gave him a tenner then climbed back in the car.

'Someone wants her bad, Jim-boy.'

Letellier pressed the throttle and we drew away.

*

Letellier and Eleanor waited for me in the Ford while I rang my answering machine. I've got a little gadget, a wonder of science, which makes the answering machine talk to me. On this occasion it didn't talk much, just two very cryptic messages; one from Maher, only he didn't announce himself, 'You were right, Jimmy, and it's all very dirty. Watch your back and call me as soon as you get this message.' This referred to Roberts, and meant that he'd been playing Bianchi's game for ten years or so, which is what I'd suggested to Maher. The second was an American voice and it simply left a phone number. I rang the number, which gave out the tell-tale code for a payphone.

'This is Jenner.'

'You have something we want, Jenner. Now we have something you want. Bring what we want to Regent's Park, by the zoo.'

'The girl?'

'Yes.'

'What have you got that I want?'

'Lucas. Bring the girl or I'll have her sent back in parcels. Several.'

'How will I know you?'

'I'll know you. Come in your Rover, we've all seen that. Go in the Gloucester gate and park by the zoo. We'll find you. No cops and no tricks, now. Send the Frenchman home. Just you and the girl.'

In the booth next to me a man was arguing with his wife or lover or something. Something about fidelity. My booth had messages scrawled all over it, also about fidelity.

'What time?'

'Eight.'

'Okay, eight. Don't hurt her.'

'You just get there, that's all you have to do, smart-arse.'

I just get there. Why's he so upset? I went back out to the car, stood next to the driver's door. More police cars passed, nee-naw, nee-naw. They make me flinch.

'I'll drive now.'

'I thought it hurt your leg?'

'It does, but I know where we're going.'

Letellier got out. I slipped behind the wheel and started the engine. I pulled away just before he reached the passenger door.

'What are you doing?' Eleanor asked.

'I wonder myself. Sometimes I do. Keep your hands where I can see them, young lady, and on no account reach under the seat because I'm feeling rather easily upset.'

She reached forward and touched my neck. I shivered.

'He's convinced you're a willing participant in all this,' I said.

'And you?'

'Talk me out of it.'

Chapter Thirty-six

I sat with Eleanor on a green-painted bench on Primrose Hill. We watched the kids and the dog-walkers go past, then we watched a misty London dusk begin to settle, painted now by a light hand, a pastoral shifting light that didn't belong to London at all. We sat beside each other and grew a little colder. I said, 'I can't make up my mind if you planned this from the beginning with Maggiera or if he just conned you with Paulo and then you were opportunist and thought, "This'll do me. Why not? This is exciting." I can't make up my mind which.'

'No. I see what you mean. Isn't that the zoo?'

'Yes.'

'Will we go down there?'

'I don't know. What do you want?'

'I don't know, either.'

'He could welcome you with open arms, and all that that means. Is that what you want?'

She shook her head.

'Or he might see you and me as the last pieces in the puzzle. If we're eliminated, click! He's got it all and no one to say otherwise. Do you think he'll do that?'

'Yes . . . but there's Leila, isn't there?'

'Yes.'

'Then we'd better turn up.'

'Why worry about her? You didn't care about Paulo, or Renan. What was Renan's crime, that she'd seen you with Maggiera? So he came and shot them both; *both*. Only your father was lucky because you were there, I think, or at least you knew what was happening and Maggiera just made it look bad. He wasn't trying to kill Charlie. I think if Charlie had been shot dead I wouldn't have given much credence to the evidence against you. No I wouldn't. But now it's open and shut, all you can tell me is when you actually decided you were in it with him.'

'That's why you wanted to know if I'd been to the South of France recently. Nice, you meant. Had I been in Nice.'

'That's right.'

She stood and walked a way down the hill, then stopped. I followed and caught her up.

'You start to feel as if everyone's suspicious, as if everyone's following you, Jimmy.'

'Nineteen?'

She smiled and kissed my cheek. 'Nearly twenty. A few months, anyway.' She walked all the way down to my Rover, then stood by it waiting for me. She sat in the passenger seat, smoking a cigarette, then said, 'Let's go and get her.'

I laid one of Leon's shotguns on my lap. It was cut short, maybe twelve inches long in the barrel. I had Eleanor's pistol in my left pocket. I kept the handle of the shotgun near my left hand. I started the engine and drove to the zoo. On the Outer Circle of Regent's Park there are big plane trees, and the big trees made the dusk look more advanced. Cars drove past. I put a newspaper over the gun for the benefit of strollers. Time passed. We sat in silence. Then a Mercedes stopped on the other side of the street from us, and suddenly there was no traffic, and suddenly I was looking at Maggiera's face; twenty-five, thirty feet away. He was in the back seat with Leila. Two men sat in the front. The windows of the Mercedes were open.

'Nice suit. You look good in it,' Maggiera called. 'It was a good buy.'

'Thank you. Now let her go.'

Maggiera let the passenger door furthest from me click open. Eleanor put her hand in my pocket. I grabbed the hand but she said, 'Let go or I'll fire it.'

I held on for a just a second longer.

'You know he *may* just want you back so he can kill you.'

'Of course he does.'

I let go. Eleanor rose from my car with the gun concealed by her side. Leila stood too.

'No funny business, Maggiera,' I called. 'I have a gun here

and you'll be the one that gets it if anything funny happens.'

He smiled and raised his hands above the blue-painted door of the Merc. Eleanor began to cross the road. So did Leila, almost touching as they passed each other. When Leila reached the bonnet of my car the Merc's driver sat back in his seat and raised a pistol. I saw the barrel for a second, then there was a sharp crack and he fell back on to his passenger. Cars passed but people didn't seem to notice us. Smoke drifted from Eleanor's pistol. She yelled at Maggiera and the passenger and they got out, dragging the driver with them and laying him on the pavement. Eleanor made them lie too, then frisked them. My passenger door opened and Leila climbed in.

'Are you okay?' she asked. 'Where's the hat?' It made me smile. Now Eleanor threw a gun into the bushes and shepherded Maggiera and his companion across the road to my car.

'Get in the back,' she said. 'Get in.'

Maggiera's companion was a tall slim man with his hair dyed blond. His knees dug into my back as he settled in the Rover. I almost said 'Well done, Eleanor,' but when I looked up again she had the pistol trained on my face.

'Hand out the shotgun, Jimmy.'

'No.'

Now I saw it.

'Give me the gun.'

'I can't let you.'

She began to squeeze the trigger. I passed out the gun, butt first.

'Give me the car keys.'

I gave her the keys.

'Now wind the windows up and push the buttons down on the doors.'

We wound the windows up.

Eleanor turned her back on us and walked over to the Merc. Eleanor stood by it for a second and I took a good long look at her and her at me. She was beautiful, okay, in her prime of beauty. Then she opened the Merc's door and got behind the wheel. The door made a soft clunk as it closed. Eleanor trained her pistol on me one last time and called, 'Don't try to move till I'm gone. If you do...'

Her voice was strange, thickened by the glass. She started the Merc's engine and moved quickly away. Maggiera had obviously figured it too, and he went into a blind panic to open the door. He wasn't fast enough. In my mirror I saw the brake lights on the Merc come on, then Eleanor's head twisted back to look at us. I was sure she raised her hand to wave. Then the Mercedes exploded, first a little one, then a ball of yellow flame as the petrol tank went. The flame grew in the soft dusk light and the Merc had been thrown slightly askew, so that it blocked the road. Maggiera was out and running, his dyed-blond friend too. I let them run. What should I do?

'What the hell was *that*?' said Leila.

I shrugged. I couldn't begin to tell her. I got out of the car and she did too. The Merc was burning now. A car stopped and a man got out. The tank blew again and he staggered back. Smoke rose between the trees. Birds shrieked in the zoo. Nearby a woman screamed.

'Let's go for a walk, Leila,' I said. 'Give me my hat.' I picked up Leon's other shotgun, wiggling it free from under my driving seat. I had his box of shells too.

'Can't we do something for her?'

I put the shotgun on my shoulder, soldier-style with the barrel pointing to the sky. We crossed the road, past the Mercedes driver. He lay on his face and bled into the gutter. On the canal bridge I stopped and threw Leon's shooter in, plus his shells. They splashed once, then disappeared with only a ripple to show they'd ever existed. Like us. Leila took my arm and we began to walk into Camden. It's a nice walk from the park, and it was a fine evening for walking.